Our CANADIAN *Girl*

Emily

JULIE LAWSON

PUFFIN
CANADA

PUFFIN CANADA

Published by the Penguin Group

Penguin Group (Canada), 90 Eglinton Avenue East, Suite 700, Toronto, Ontario, Canada M4P 2Y3
(a division of Pearson Canada Inc.)

Penguin Group (USA) Inc., 375 Hudson Street, New York, New York 10014, U.S.A.
Penguin Books Ltd, 80 Strand, London WC2R 0RL, England
Penguin Ireland, 25 St Stephen's Green, Dublin 2, Ireland (a division of Penguin Books Ltd)
Penguin Group (Australia), 250 Camberwell Road, Camberwell, Victoria 3124, Australia
(a division of Pearson Australia Group Pty Ltd)
Penguin Books India Pvt Ltd, 11 Community Centre, Panchsheel Park, New Delhi – 110 017, India
Penguin Group (NZ), 67 Apollo Drive, Rosedale, North Shore 0632, New Zealand
(a division of Pearson New Zealand Ltd)
Penguin Books (South Africa) (Pty) Ltd, 24 Sturdee Avenue, Rosebank,
Johannesburg 2196, South Africa

Penguin Books Ltd, Registered Offices: 80 Strand, London WC2R 0RL, England

First published 2010

1 2 3 4 5 6 7 8 9 10 (WEB)

Emily: Across the James Bay Bridge copyright © Julie Lawson, 2001
Emily: Disaster at the Bridge copyright © Julie Lawson, 2002
Emily: Building Bridges copyright © Julie Lawson, 2003
Emily: Summer of Gold copyright © Julie Lawson, 2004

Design: Matthews Communications Design Inc.
Interior illustrations copyright © Janet Wilson
Map and chapter-opening illustrations copyright © Sharon Matthews

Manufactured in Canada.

LIBRARY AND ARCHIVES CANADA CATALOGUING IN PUBLICATION

Lawson, Julie, 1947–
Emily / Julie Lawson.

(Our Canadian girl)
A compilation of four previously published titles : Across
the James Bay bridge, 2001; Disaster at the bridge, 2002;
Building bridges, 2003; and Summer of gold, 2004.
ISBN 978-0-14-317085-3

1. Victoria (B.C.)—History—Juvenile fiction.
I. Title. II. Series: Our Canadian girl.

PS8573.A933E44 2010   jC813'.54   C2010-901627-0

Visit the Penguin Group (Canada) website at www.penguin.ca

Special and corporate bulk purchase rates available; please see
www.penguin.ca/corporatesales or call 1-800-810-3104, ext. 2477 or 2474

To Charlayne Thornton-Joe for her tireless commitment to "building bridges"

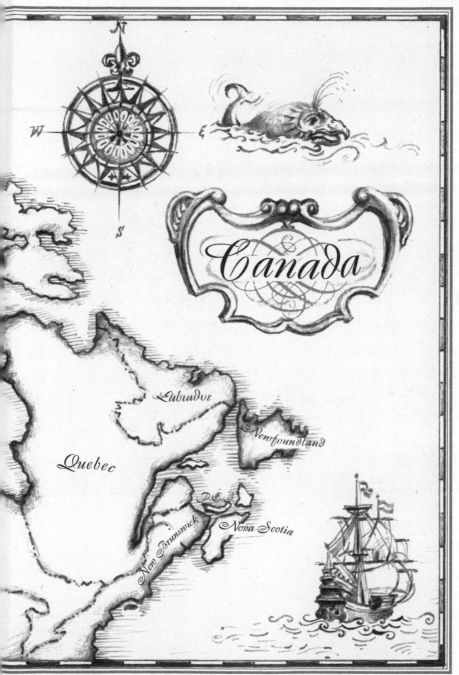

Canada

Labrador

Newfoundland

Quebec

P.E.I.

New Brunswick

Nova Scotia

Marks the location of the story

MEET EMILY

THE YEAR IS 1896. THE PLACE IS VICTORIA, BRITISH Columbia. The young girl you're about to meet is ten year old Emily Murdoch.

Emily and her two younger sisters were born in the Dominion of Canada, but her parents came from England, in the 1880s. They settled in a Victoria neighbourhood called James Bay, a residential area popular with working-class, middle-class, and upper-class families. It is also an industrial area, with factories, shipyards, and an ocean dock that could accommodate large vessels.

Emily's father works in a bank, and she and her sisters enjoy a comfortable, middle-class lifestyle. Like other girls her age, Emily goes to school and church, and enjoys playing with her friends.

By 1889, Victoria was the largest and wealthiest city in the province. Its location, on the southeastern tip of

Vancouver Island, made it a commercial centre for foreign trade, and the first available seaport north of San Francisco. It housed the provincial government, the Royal Navy, and the second-largest iron-works on the Pacific coast. It was a large manufacturing centre, and boasted an assortment of activities related to forestry, fishing, sealing, agriculture, and commerce.

During Emily's ten years, the Esquimalt and Nanaimo Railway had arrived in town, electric lighting was introduced, and mail was delivered to her door twice a day—free. Recent improvements in the city water works provided residents with an abundant supply of pure water, ample for fire protection as well as domestic use. The city had a sewage system, indoor plumbing, and an expanding streetcar service.

Victoria also had a touch of the exotic. In the early 1880s, several shiploads of Chinese people were brought to British Columbia to work on the Fraser Canyon section of the new Canadian Pacific Railway. When the construction was complete, thousands settled in Victoria's Chinatown. Many found employment as cooks, servants, or gardeners in Victorian households such as Emily's.

Although Chinese New Year celebrations and funeral processions fascinated some white residents, anti-Chinese sentiments were still the rule of the day. In 1885, the federal government introduced a fifty-dollar head tax on every Chinese person entering the country, in an attempt to control Chinese immigration.

As 1896 is ushered in, the world around Emily is beginning to change. An increasing shortage of gold had led to panic in 1893 and a worldwide financial depression had followed. Emily is unaware of the effect this might have on her family. She expects life to go on as usual—with some new friends, perhaps, and new adventures. She hopes she'll get society's latest craze—a bicycle. But what does the new year really have in store for her?

Turn the page and read on!

BOOK ONE

*Across the
James Bay Bridge*

CHAPTER N⁰ 1

The first day of 1896 blew in with a bitter wind and the threat of snow. In spite of the cold, Emily and her younger sister Jane were happy to be outside in Beacon Hill Park.

Things were bustling at home. Ten guests would be arriving later that afternoon for the Murdochs' annual New Year's party. A few of those guests had already sent ahead their Chinese servants to help Hing prepare the dinner, and Mother and Father were making sure that everything was perfect, down to the last detail. Because the girls kept getting in the way, Mother had sent four-year-old Amelia to bed for a nap and told Jane and Emily they could go to the park and feed the ducks—provided they dressed warmly and hurried home the instant they heard the gong.

The ducks were used to the girls' weekly offerings and quickly gathered around. But when a mob of seagulls squawked in for their share, Emily would have none of it. "Shoo!" she yelled. She ran in circles, flinging her arms in an attempt to scare them away. "This is a *duck* pond!"

"Look, Em!" Jane called out. She had several of the ducks trying to eat out of her hand. "One of them's pecking my finger."

"You chase the gulls for a while and let me feed them," Emily said, racing over to her sister. She took some grain from the small bag that Jane was carrying, moved a few yards away, then crouched down and held out two handfuls. "Here, ducks! Over here!"

"Over *here*!" Jane countered. Soon they were

deeply involved in a contest over who could attract the greater number.

Suddenly, the clamour of a gong echoed across the park.

"Oh, no!" Emily cried. "Is it that time already? Come on, Jane. We've got to go home." She scattered the remaining feed and grabbed her sister's hand.

Emily was used to Hing's gong. Before he'd started using it, she had always arrived late for lunch on school days. Hing had finally laid down the law. "I stand outside, beat gong when dinner ready," he'd said. "If you not here, you miss."

The gong outdid the clanging of the streetcar and could be heard throughout James Bay. The moment Emily heard it, she would stop whatever she was doing and run like the dickens. She didn't want to make Hing angry. If he was angry, there would be no lemon tarts!

No, the gong was not to be taken lightly—not on regular days, not on New Year's Day, and certainly not when Father was home.

Home was only three blocks from the park. But as the girls were nearing the end of the second block, Emily spotted something that made her forget the gong and come to an abrupt stop.

"Oh, Jane!"

"What?"

"See, on Sullivans' verandah? The bicycle." She leaned over the picket fence and sighed. "It's a Red Bird. That's what I wanted for Christmas."

"Maybe you'll get one for your birthday," Jane said. "It's not that far away." She gave Emily an encouraging smile and continued on home.

Emily stared at the bicycle. A birthday present? Jane could be right. Father had often said that a tenth birthday was extra special.

Another clanging of the gong tore her away. She could picture Father pulling out his watch, his foot tapping with impatience. Of course, once she had her bicycle, she would always be on time.

CHAPTER N°2

Father was waiting at the door, watch in hand.
"Quickly, girls! The guests will be arriving in forty-five minutes. We want you scrubbed and polished." He smiled.

"Did you polish your gold tooth, Father?" Emily asked. "It's gleaming."

"Of course, my dear. You can't start a new year without giving everything a special shine. So off you go! And mind you don't dawdle."

"No, Father." She raced Jane upstairs to the bathroom for the required scrubbing.

Amelia, who looked as polished as a new penny, came in to supervise. "Don't forget your ears and your fingernails," she said. "Mother will check."

After their bath, they went to their room and found their best clothes neatly laid out on the bed.

Emily reached for her stockings. "Do you remember last year's party, Jane? There won't be as many people this year, but it will be even better because some *new* people are coming! They just arrived from England. Mr. Walsh works in the bank with Father. They've got one son in the Royal Navy and one son who's eleven. His name is George."

"How do you know? And you'd better hurry. I'm already dressed."

Emily put on her petticoat, then reached for her frilly white dress. "I know because they bought the house next door to Alice." Alice was Emily's closest friend.

Just then Mother came in, her silk dress swishing across the floor. "Still not ready? Oh,

Emily! You know how your father likes things to run smoothly." She fastened the mother-of-pearl buttons on Emily's dress, then turned her attention to her hair.

Emily squirmed and wriggled but at last the ordeal was over: starched dress done up, long curls brushed out, red velvet sash tied around her waist, matching ribbon in her hair. After her hands and fingernails—and ears—were examined, she had only to put on her shoes and go downstairs.

One by one the guests arrived. They gathered in both the sitting room and the parlour, chatting over glasses of punch while warming themselves by the fire.

Emily waited excitedly for the newcomer, George. She wanted to show him around the house and tell him about the school he'd be attending once the holidays were over. But when he and his parents arrived, there wasn't time. Dinner was announced. The guests made their way into the dining room in a leisurely fashion and took their places at the long table.

Mother had seated George and Emily side by side.

"Your neighbour, Alice, told me all about you," Emily said.

George gave her a mischievous grin. "Her brother, Tom, told me all about *you*."

"Oh, no!" Emily giggled and hid her face so he wouldn't see her blushing.

After Father said grace, Hing brought in the plates and began to serve, helped out on this occasion by a neighbour's housemaid. The first course was oyster pie, followed by a clear soup. Then came chicken and tongue and cold boiled ham, with mixed pickles and celery, onions in cream sauce, and two types of potatoes: sweet potatoes with brown sugar, mashed potatoes with gravy. Emily noticed that George was tucking in heartily, but she was careful to save room for dessert.

Finally Hing brought in the flaming plum pudding. Emily savoured every bite, especially the hard sauce poured over top.

It was a long time to sit minding your manners. Emily didn't realize how much she'd been fidgeting until she caught Father's eye. She immediately stopped pleating her linen napkin and folded her hands in her lap. She glanced at Mother, hoping to be excused from the table, but Mother shook her head and mouthed the word "toasts."

The dreaded toasts. Emily sighed loudly and slumped in her chair, prompting another stern look from Father.

Then, at last, Father was on his feet, wineglass in hand. "The Queen!" he said. Everyone stood up, raised his glass, and repeated, "The Queen!"

Emily and George were over eight years old, so they were each given a half glass of white wine. George downed his in one gulp, then made a spectacle of himself by coughing. Emily knew better—the stuff tasted horrid—so she merely touched the glass to her lips and pretended to drink.

No sooner had the Queen been toasted than Mr. Walsh stood and proposed a toast to their hostess. Once again everyone stood and raised his glass, this time to Mother. Then it was Father's turn. Stand, raise glass, sit down. Happy New Year, good health .... And so it went, round the table, with toasts to everyone.

Emily wished she could propose a marmalade instead of a toast. A marmalade to Jane and Amelia. Or why not to George? She glanced at him and stifled a giggle. With his reddish-brown hair, perhaps she ought to propose a strawberry jam!

The toasts dragged on. At last, when Emily had had all the stands and sits she could take, Father allowed the children to be excused.

"We're going to play Happy New Year with our dolls," Jane said.

"You can play, too, Em," said Amelia. "And George can make the toasts."

Emily shook her head. "We're going to have a tour of the house."

She grabbed George's hand, taking him very much by surprise, and they made their getaway up the staircase.

She proudly showed him the new bathroom, with its indoor flush toilet and claw-foot tub. Next came the play room, where her sisters' dolls were sitting down to their New Year's feast. After a quick peek inside her parents' bedroom, they went into the room Emily shared with her sisters. It was large and bright with a window seat that overlooked the street.

"I can watch everything from here," she said. "I can see when my friends are coming, and the postman and the milkman. And what the Chinese peddlers are selling."

"Chinese peddlers?" George turned up his nose.

"Haven't you seen them? They balance a bamboo pole on their shoulders and hang a basket at each end. They go from house to house all over Victoria. Some of them sell vegetables or fish, and some collect the laundry. I can watch the streetcar, too. It's electric! It goes right down our street and stops at the next block.

Wait till you hear it! The bell clangs and the over-head wires whistle and the conductor shouts hello to everyone. It takes you anywhere in the city for five cents."

Back on the main floor, they looked into the kitchen, where the Chinese servants were washing the dishes. One man paused above a vat of boiling water and caught sight of Emily.

"Em-ry!" he called out. "*Gung hey fat choy.*"

"*Gung hey fat choy!*" she replied. "That's Hing," she told George. "He's teaching me some Chinese."

George grunted. "Don't tell me you understand that *hey choy* nonsense."

"It's what the Chinese say for Happy New Year. But their new year is different from ours."

"What's 'Em-ry,' then?"

"My name, silly! He calls Alice 'A-ris.'"

"Barbarians," George muttered.

"Didn't you have a Chinese servant in England?"

George gave her a horrified look. "We had English servants, of course."

"What's in this room?" He stopped before a door at the end of the hall.

"That's Father's study. We're not allowed in unless—George!"

He was already inside, gazing at a vast collection of objects displayed in a large glass cabinet. "What's all this?"

"Father's antiquities," Emily explained. "They're from the Far East. Father got some on his travels and some were gifts. See the vase with the dragon?" She pointed to a blue-and-white porcelain vase. "It only just arrived. My uncle in London sent it. Father says it's eight hundred years old."

"Is that a real dagger beside it?" George asked. "I say! It looks like a ram's head on the handle. Can I have a closer look?"

"No!" Emily cried in alarm. "What are you doing? You can't touch it!" She reached out to stop him. As she did so, her arm brushed the vase and sent it crashing to the floor.

"Oh, no!" she gasped. Her stomach churned.

What would Father say?

"I don't think anyone heard," George said. "Do you?"

"I don't know." Her mouth felt so dry she could hardly speak.

"At least *I* didn't break it," George went on. "You're in for it now. Would you like me to tell your father? Might make it easier."

She shook her head, wishing she could die on the spot.

"Suit yourself," George said. "Shall we go back upstairs and spy on your sisters?" Before she could answer, he was gone.

With shaking fingers, Emily picked up the broken pieces. Part of the vase was still intact. If it were facing out . . . She propped it on the shelf and hid the other pieces in behind. It looked a little tippy, but it would have to do for now. Tonight she would not pray for a bicycle. She would pray that Father stay out of his study for a very long time.

She left the study and closed the door. As

she was passing the dining room she heard her father say, "A toast—to better times."

Emily couldn't help but agree.

Then Father continued, "Not to put a damper on the festivities, but I cannot help worrying about this economic slump and its outcome. I fear we may have some tough times ahead."

Emily frowned. The broken vase certainly meant tough times for *her* once Father found out. But what did "tough times" mean for him and his guests? He worked in the bank, so perhaps it had to do with money. And if *that* were the case, maybe that was why she didn't get a bicycle for Christmas.

No, that couldn't be right. Father had no end of money. Like Jane said, he was saving the bicycle for her birthday. The thought made her smile . . . until she remembered the vase.

And later, when everyone was joining hands and singing "Auld Lang Syne," Emily had but one thought: How could she put it back together?

CHAPTER N° 3

As luck would have it, it snowed overnight.
Father shovelled the verandah steps and then left
right away for his usual walk to the bank. Mother
went outside with Jane and Amelia to help them
build a snowman. Emily stayed inside. With Hing
having the day off, she had the house to herself.

She had a plan, but she had to act quickly. First
she needed glue. What kind of glue worked with
porcelain? Surely not the ordinary paste she used
for paper. She needed something strong, something hard. . . . Mother's hard sauce! Mother

often made glue with flour and water but it was lumpy. The sauce was smooth. And when it was dry it went hard, like frosting on a cake.

She dashed to the kitchen and flipped through the pages of her mother's book, the *Household Companion*, until she found the recipe. Butter, powdered sugar, brandy. She put some sugar in a bowl, added the butter, and beat it into a thick, smooth paste.

She couldn't find the brandy, but she figured a colourless liquid labelled "alcohol" would do the trick. She stirred in a few drops. The smell was so horrid she decided not to taste it. Besides, her sauce was not for pudding.

She hurried into the study and removed the broken vase. There were about ten pieces, and some were rather large. Taking one piece at a time, she applied the glue to the broken edges. Then, with trembling fingers, she fit the pieces together.

She was wiping away the smudges when she heard her sisters calling at the back door. "Emily, get us a carrot! Our snowman needs a nose! And Mother says to hurry!"

"Coming!" she cried. She returned the vase to the cabinet and gave it one last look. The blue lines of the dragon matched up, and the glue appeared to be holding. Unless Father examined the vase closely, he would never know.

The snow kept Emily's mind off the vase and her father out of his study. Victoria didn't get much snow, and Emily couldn't miss the opportunity to go sledding with her friends. As for Father, as soon as he got home from work, he took the whole family to Beacon Hill Park for sleigh rides with friends and neighbours. For two afternoons and evenings the streets rang with sleigh bells instead of the clanging streetcars.

On the third night of the new year, Emily was awakened by a dreadful shaking. The whole house rocked. Windows rattled and glassware jingled. When the shaking finally stopped, Mother and Father rushed in to calm the frightened girls.

"It was an earthquake," said Father. "It's all over now."

The next day they learned that the earthquake had lasted fifteen seconds and had been felt throughout Victoria. "It was quite severe," Father told them, "but there was no serious damage."

Emily thought of the vase. If it were discovered now, they could blame the earthquake. "Did anything get broken?" she asked. "Any dishes or . . . vases?"

"Not so much as an egg cup," Mother said. "The only thing that shattered was our nerves."

"Not even the slightest crack?" Emily persisted.

Father ruffled her hair. "What a worrier you

are! There wasn't the tiniest splinter."

"Our snowman got broke," Amelia said glumly.

"You can blame that on the rain," Father said. "There'll be no sleigh rides today."

Jane sniffed. "And no more snow."

"But there might be another earthquake?" Emily tried to keep her voice from sounding too hopeful.

"No, dear." Mother gave her a hug. "You'll sleep peacefully tonight."

CHAPTER N° 4

"Go on, Emily!" George gave her a poke. "Sneak up and pull his pigtail."

From her hiding place behind the hedge in front of George's house, Emily watched the peddler jog-trotting along the muddy street. He was a familiar sight, dressed in dark, baggy trousers, a loose-fitting jacket, and a wide-brimmed hat. And like the other Chinese men, he wore his hair in a long pigtail.

"He's not going to bite you," Alice said. "George pulled a peddler's pigtail yesterday.

Tom and I did too."

"We dare you," George went on. "If you're not too much of a scaredy-cat."

Emily frowned. She didn't want to do it. If Hing found out, he wouldn't like it one bit.

Still, she didn't take dares lightly. And as for being a scaredy-cat? They'd see about that.

She ran up behind the peddler and gave his pigtail a good hard tug. He whirled around and shouted as she fled back to the hedge.

"He sure looked mad." Alice laughed. "Did you see him shaking his fist? He probably put a curse on you."

"Where does he live?" George asked.

"In Chinatown, where else?" said Alice. "Mother says it stinks to high heaven of sharks' fins and rotten eggs."

"You must mean thousand-year-old eggs," Emily said. "They're not really that old, and they're not rotten. They're preserved. They're dark purple on the outside and green inside."

"How do you know?" said Tom.

"Hing brought me one to taste. It was good."

The others groaned with disgust. "You wouldn't catch me eating that rubbish," George said. "And I'd never set foot in Chinatown."

"Me neither," said Alice. "Would you, Em?"

"Yes!" Emily suddenly felt very bold. "In fact, I think I might go this very afternoon. And I dare all of you to come with me."

"You can't be serious," said Tom.

"Why not? I went once before, with Father. And it's not as bad as you make out. So . . . I double dare you."

Alice shook her head. "Our parents would never allow it."

"They wouldn't need to know," Emily continued, warming to her plan. "We'll ask if we can go across the bridge into town. We could even do some errands and get candy at the grocer's." When the others still hesitated, she burst out, "You're brave enough to pull a peddler's pigtail but you won't even go to Chinatown? You only have to stay a minute. I triple dare you!" She glared at George. "If you don't, I'll tell Father you went snooping into his room. When *I* told you not to!"

George rolled his eyes. "Oh, very well. Let's all go. It might be a lark. If we remember to plug our noses."

Everyone received permission for the trip to town, and shortly after lunch they were ready to go. Mother told Emily to be back for tea and to bring home some candy for her sisters. "Behave yourself," she said. "And stay on the boardwalks. The roads are a frightful mess."

A brisk walk down Birdcage Walk led them to the wooden bridge that spanned James Bay. As they stepped onto the bridge, Emily pulled a face. "Eugh! Low tide!"

"It stinks here all the time," said Alice.

A stream of foam came spewing out of the soap-works factory on the far shore. It floated onto the mud flats and mingled with the garbage and debris that people often dumped in the bay.

"I like it at high tide," said Emily. "In the summer, Father rents a rowboat and takes us under the bridge."

Once they crossed the bridge, they headed up Government Street. Horse-drawn hacks stood one behind the other, waiting for fares. The streetcar whistled by at a good ten miles an hour.

They passed the Bank of B.C. where Emily's father worked, several dry-goods stores, a clothier's, a butcher's, and the post office. When they reached the grocer's, they hurried inside for their candy. Everything was out in the open, from hams and bacon to barrels of English biscuits and enormous rounds of cheese. Emily counted out a penny's worth of lemon barley sugar sticks and butter taffy drops, making sure she had enough for her sisters.

They left the grocer's and continued up the street. But as they were crossing the Johnson Street ravine, they heard a series of explosions that stopped them in their tracks.

"That sounds like firecrackers!" George exclaimed. "Where are they coming from?"

"Chinatown," Emily said. "We're almost there."

They reached the end of the footbridge, walked a short distance in the mud, then turned into Chinatown.

The street was crowded with Chinese people, chatting in small groups or hurrying along with their bamboo poles. A string of firecrackers, tied in tight red clusters, hung from a wooden balcony all the way down to the boardwalk below. Someone had lit the string at the lower end, and the fire was steadily popping its way to the top.

"Let's take the rest!" said George. "We can set them off in the park!" He grabbed the string and yanked it from the balcony. Then he stamped out the fire, scooped up the unlit firecrackers, and ran off.

"Stop!" someone shouted. Several men gave chase.

"Down here!" Emily cried. She ducked into a narrow brick alley, assuming the others were close behind. But when she stopped for breath, she found she was alone. Where were they? Surely they wouldn't have run off and left her.

She continued down the alley, not daring to return to the street with all the shouting going on. That George! she thought angrily. It's his fault. If I have to go home by myself . . .

The alley had begun to twist and turn, with numerous paths branching off in different directions. Emily followed one after another. Finally, with no end in sight, she realized she would have to retrace her steps.

"I hope you're satisfied, George!" she fumed. "Mr. Know-it-all!" Then anxiously, "How do I get out of here?"

Just then, who should appear but Hing.

"Em-ry?" He frowned. "What are you doing here?"

"Oh, Hing!" Her words came out in a rush. "I didn't want to pull his pigtail but they dared me. So then I dared them to come to Chinatown, especially that George, who's always getting into trouble. First it was Father's study and the vase—and it was *his* fault I broke it! And then he stole the firecrackers. That's why we ran off. I came down the alley to hide—" A thought struck her. "Is it Chinese New Year already? Is that why there are firecrackers?"

"No, no. New Year next month. Firecrackers for open new store. To scare away evil spirits and bring good fortune."

"Oh." She gave him a worried look. "Why aren't you still at my house?" He'd been there that morning, cooking the traditional Saturday roast so they could have cold pork on Sunday. "Your half day is Sunday, isn't it? Are you sick?"

"No, no. Change half day, one time. Today—" His words were interrupted by a loud banging. "Come!" He took her hand and led her back to the street.

A large and noisy procession was moving through Chinatown. Cymbals crashed. Women cried and wailed. They even held bowls under their eyes to catch the tears.

"What kind of parade is that?" Emily asked. "And why are all those people wearing white?"

"Funeral," Hing said. "Friend from home village." He told Emily he'd take her as far as the James Bay bridge, but then he would join the procession himself.

By the time they turned down Government, the street was lined with curious onlookers.

"There's Alice, up ahead," Emily said. "And Tom and George. Thank goodness, he doesn't have the firecrackers any more." She handed Hing a butter taffy drop and ran to join her friends.

CHAPTER № 5

At school on Monday, Emily was faced with a barrage of questions. "Where's your bicycle?" her classmates asked. "You said you were getting one for Christmas."

"It's going to be a birthday present," she told them.

"How do you know for sure? What kind are you getting? Will you let us ride it sometimes?"

She answered the questions as best she could, until, much to her relief, her teacher rang the bell.

As she was walking home at noon, she once again spotted the Red Bird bicycle. This time, it was leaning against the side of the Sullivans' house.

No one was about. She went over to the bicycle and touched the smooth frame. She spun the pedals and gripped the handlebars. She clambered onto the leather seat, bracing herself against the wall. Even though her feet didn't quite reach the pedals, she closed her eyes and pretended she was flying along Dallas Road with the sea breeze in her hair. It was one of the Ten Commandments not to covet anything that belonged to a neighbour, but oh, how she coveted that bicycle! Only three weeks until her birthday. Maybe Father had already bought her bicycle. Maybe he was hiding it in the bank, away from prying eyes.

When her imaginary ride was over, she hopped off and daringly rang the little bell attached to the handlebars. Its brassy tinkle reminded her that she hadn't heard Hing's gong.

She gave the bicycle one last pat and hurried on, thinking she was either very early or extremely late.

At home, she was astonished to find her sisters bickering in the breakfast room, her mother in a panic in the kitchen, and no meal in sight.

"Emily, where have you been?" Mother cried.

Without waiting for an answer, she thrust a plate of cold tongue sandwiches into Emily's hands. "Put this on the table and come back for the milk. It never rains but it pours. Today of all days, with guests coming for tea."

"It's not raining!" Amelia squealed. "Mother, you said it was raining and pouring!"

"Hush, Amelia, and eat! You, too, Jane. And Emily, you're going to be late for school."

Between mouthfuls, Emily said, "I saw a Red Bird bicycle on my way home. I hope I get the same kind for my birthday. I sat on the seat to try it out and it was almost my size. It was rather high, but I don't think it's all that difficult to lower the seat. Won't it be grand, Mother? I'll never be late, and Hing won't ever have to bang the gong again. Where is he, anyway?"

"Oh, Emily! I'm so sorry, I know how fond you are of Hing—"

"Mother, what's happened? Is he all right?"

"When's he coming back?" Jane asked.

"Hing's hurt!" Amelia began to cry.

"No, no, it's nothing like that," Mother said reassuringly. "Girls, your father dismissed Hing this morning. He acted in haste, and I'm sure he'll regret it and make amends, but meanwhile—oh, Amelia, let Jane pour your milk, you're going to knock it over—meanwhile, the ladies will be here sharp at two o'clock and nothing's prepared!"

Emily had never seen her mother in such a state. "I'll stay home and help," she offered.

"Me too!" said Jane. "If Emily misses school, can I?"

"No, Jane."

"That's not fair!" Jane pounded the table and knocked over her milk.

"Now look what you've done! Emily, give me a hand, please."

The next several minutes were filled with crying and confusion. But soon Amelia was in bed for a nap and Jane was on her way back to school. Mother mixed batter for scones. And after clearing the table and wiping the spilt milk, Emily was set to work making egg salad sandwiches.

"What about Hing?" she asked as she sliced the bread. "Will he be here tomorrow? He promised he'd make lemon tarts tomorrow. Why did Father dismiss him? Mother—"

"Emily, please! It's all very distressing, and I'll explain in due course, but now is simply not the time. Oh, dear, look at the bread! We want thin straight across, not sloping. And for goodness' sake, don't slice your finger."

Before long, the thick-and-thin sandwiches were on a plate, the scones were in the oven, and the guests were sipping tea in the parlour.

Emily was filling a cut-glass bowl with strawberry preserves to go with the scones when she heard Hing's name. Curious, she crept down the hall and, sucking on a spoonful of preserves, put her ear to the parlour door. She was just in time to hear her mother say, ". . . discovered it broken and dismissed him this morning."

Emily gasped in disbelief. Hing could not have been dismissed because of the vase. He knew that *she* was responsible. Surely he would have said something.

"The blue and white porcelain vase," her mother went on. "Yesterday afternoon, before we went to the church social, I asked Hing to do a thorough cleaning in Robert's study. There's been the most peculiar smell of rubbing alcohol. Well, as he was cleaning the shelves in the display case, he must have dropped the vase."

"You can't trust them." Emily recognized the voice of George's mother, Mrs. Walsh. "I know it's the custom in Victoria, but I certainly wouldn't have a Chinaman in my house."

"But he's an excellent servant!" Mother exclaimed. "Ten years he's been with us, since

Emily was a baby, and not a speck of trouble."

"What did he have to say for himself?"

"Nothing. He remained absolutely silent."

Emily's stomach lurched. Hing had been dismissed because of her, and he hadn't let on . . .

"Who else could it have been?" Mother continued. "The girls are forbidden to go into the study."

"You should have hired an English servant from the start," Mrs. Walsh said. "They're much more reliable."

"Nonsense!" someone retorted. "Not any of the girls I've had. They stay for a month, then they're off getting married. No, the Orientals are definitely the best, provided you train them properly and keep an eye on them. I was saying the other day . . . excuse me, Anne, I don't mean to be rude, but is something burning?"

"Oh, mercy!" Emily bolted back to the kitchen, her mother close behind. She flung open the oven door and gagged as smoke billowed into the room. Then she grabbed the oven mitts and pulled out the blackened mess. There would be no scones served with thick cream and strawberry preserves today.

"Whatever were you thinking?" Mother spoke sharply, but sounded more exasperated than angry.

Emily tried to keep her voice from trembling. "Mother, I'm sorry. I promise I'll clean up, but right now I have to go back to school because I've forgotten something important."

"Your father will hear about this!"

"I know," Emily said as she grabbed her coat and ran out. "And I'll explain everything."

First, she had to find Hing.

CHAPTER N.° 6

Emily's plan was simple. She would go to Chinatown, find Hing, and take him home with her. Once Father learned the truth about the vase, he'd likely give Emily a sound thrashing— but at least he'd give Hing back his job.

When she got to Chinatown, she turned down the same alley she'd gone into before, found the same lane, and recognized the spot where Hing had unexpectedly appeared. The problem was, where exactly had he come from?

It was different in this hidden part of

Chinatown. There were chicken coops, barking dogs, lines of washing, and gardens with winter vegetables. The tightly packed buildings bulged in on each other, sometimes three storeys high.

She walked through a courtyard and down another alley, only to reach a dead end. She tried a different route but ended up in another courtyard.

Passersby gave her curious looks. "Hing?" she asked. "Do you know Hing?" No one could help.

With a growing sense of panic, she wandered through the maze, from dead end to dead end, one courtyard to another. There were too many staircases, too many doorways. Faces peered out of windows, smoke rose from chimneys. Inside the squalid rooms, lamps were being lit. It would soon be dark. And it was starting to rain.

Just then, a peddler stepped out of a doorway. Emily was about to approach when she recognized him as the man whose pigtail she had pulled. She shuddered. She couldn't ask *him* for help. He'd think she was up to more mischief and put another curse on her. If he so much as saw her . . .

She turned too quickly, stumbled over a heap of refuse, and fell onto a jagged pile of bricks. "Oh, mercy!" A sob welled up in her throat. It was raining hard now, the wind cut through to her bones, and her hands and knees smarted horribly.

"Em-ry?"

The familiar voice made her giddy with relief.

"Oh, Hing, I'm so sorry! That vase . . . I should have told Father right away instead of trying to hide it, and now you've lost your job. So will you come home with me? I'll tell Father and he'll hire you back—" A dreadful thought struck her. What if Hing had taken another position? What if he didn't want to come back? She burst into tears. "Oh, please!"

"Come." He led her to a door a few steps away and ushered her inside a cramped and dingy room. After clearing a space for her to sit down, he poured her a cup of tea. "Drink," he said.

"Then we go home and explain."

She thanked him, then picked up the cup and frowned. The tea didn't look like proper tea; there were leaves floating on top. But she remembered her manners and took a sip. It had a slightly bitter, but pleasant taste, and it warmed her right through.

"Green tea," Hing said. "You like?"

"Yes. Thank you." As she drank the tea, she took in her surroundings—the rough pieces of furniture, a wood stove, shelves with cracked and mismatched china. On a crate beside the narrow bed she noticed a studio portrait of a young Chinese woman seated with two small boys.

"Who are they?" she wondered.

"Wife and sons." Hing smiled proudly.

"Are they in Victoria too?"

Hing's expression changed. He told Emily how he'd come to Canada in 1883 to work on the railway, hoping to earn enough money to send for his family. Two years later he'd succeeded. He'd then returned to China and spent many months visiting friends and relatives and telling them about the land they called Gold Mountain.

It was difficult to follow everything he said. He spoke slowly and all his *l*'s came out as *r*'s. But his story fascinated Emily. It was like a fairy tale, only real. Even though there was no happy ending. Hing and his family had packed their belongings for Gold Mountain only to discover that the government in Canada had established a head tax. Every Chinese entering the country had to pay fifty dollars. Hing could only afford to pay for himself.

The opportunities in Gold Mountain were so much greater than those in his homeland, he had left his wife and sons and returned to Victoria. He'd promised to send for them as soon as he could save enough money to cover their head tax.

"You must miss them," said Emily.

"I have daughter, too," he said sadly. "Born in Year of Dog. Ten years old. Like you."

"*Almost* ten," Emily reminded him. "Is she pretty, like your wife?"

"I never see her. No picture. But I think yes, she very pretty."

Emily didn't understand why Hing, who'd been working in Victoria for ten years, still hadn't saved enough money to send for his family. It would be rude to ask, but she couldn't help but wonder.

"Getting late," Hing said. "We go now."

Emily thought about his story all the way home. To think Hing had a wife and children she'd never even heard about . . . He must miss them dreadfully. And to leave Emily's cozy house, night after night, for that horrid little room . . .

She wondered if her parents knew. Well, as soon as the vase business was settled and Hing was back at work, she'd tell them. And when Father learned how lonely Hing was, he'd pay him a higher wage. Then Hing would be able to bring his family to Canada and the story would have a happy ending. Especially when Hing saw his daughter for the very first time.

CHAPTER N.º 7

Father did not look pleased when Emily came into the house. He held out his pocket watch and said sternly, "Do you see what time it is? Mother and I have been frantic. What do you have to say for yourself?"

Emily glanced over her shoulder at Hing, waiting in the doorway. Then she bowed her head and stammered, "I had to find Hing, Father. He got fired because of me. Because I broke the vase. And I was afraid to tell you."

Her parents looked at her with shocked

expressions. Before they could say anything, she rushed on.

"It was at the New Year's party and George went into your study and he wanted to see the dagger. I tried to stop him . . ." She swallowed hard to force back the tears. "I knocked over the vase and I glued it back together. Then Hing got blamed and you sent him away, and the whole time he never said it was me, even though he knew. Oh, please, Father! Please hire him back! He's got a whole family in China and a little girl—"

"That's enough for now, Emily," Father said. "Wait for me in the study. Mother and I will speak to you shortly."

The list seemed endless. Emily stood before her father, head hung in disgrace, as Mother gave a full account of the day's disasters.

"I left her with the simple task of keeping an eye on the scones. Instead, she left the kitchen and dripped strawberry preserves on the carpet. Then she stepped in it and tracked it down the hall. The scones were burnt to cinders. And what does she do then? She flies out with a story about forgetting something at school. As for the rest! Going into the study, breaking the vase— admittedly, it was an accident—and failing to say anything . . ." Mother shook her head.

Father sighed. "You did a great wrong by not telling us about the vase. But you've put things right in an admirable way. Except for the mess in the hall and kitchen, and you'll clean that up tomorrow." He then sent her sobbing to her room.

"Don't cry, Em," Jane said, giving her a hug. "Father won't stay mad for long, and you'll still get your bicycle. And—don't tell, but I was listening outside the door and I know Hing's coming back first thing tomorrow."

Emily squeezed Jane's hand. The thought of Hing in his lonely room, with no family close by for comfort, made her cry even harder.

The next evening, Emily decided to put another plan into action.

"Father," she said, "when you and Mother came to Canada did you pay a head tax?"

"Head tacks?" Amelia looked puzzled. "That would hurt."

"Not those tacks," Emily said. "Tax like what you pay. Isn't that right, Father? Did you have to pay it?"

"What? I'm sorry, dear. What did you say?"

She repeated the question.

"Englishmen paying a head tax? Certainly not!"

"Oh. But . . . I heard people had to pay fifty dollars to come into Canada."

"Only the Chinese."

"Will they always have to pay the fifty dollars?"

"Hmm? Oh. The fifty dollars. No . . ."

Emily's face lit up. Wait till she told Hing!

Then Father continued, "It's very likely the head tax will be raised to one hundred dollars. Possibly for the best. There's enough unemployment as it is."

Oh, no. Hing would have to act quickly or pay an even higher tax.

"Father, I was wondering if you could—"

"Hush, Emily!" Mother said. "Can't you see your father's tired? You girls may be excused."

Emily sighed. Her request for Hing's raise would have to wait.

CHAPTER № 8

"Happy birthday, Em!" Jane and Amelia pounced on their sister. She kissed them both and ran downstairs to the breakfast room.

"Happy birthday, dear." Father ruffled her hair. "How does it feel to be ten years old?"

"It feels grown up! Enough to cycle around the world."

Mother laughed. "You'll have to wait another few years for that. Meanwhile, sit down and eat your breakfast. Father has a surprise."

"Yes, indeed," he said. "I want you to walk to

the bank with me this morning."

"The whole way?" She often accompanied him as far as the James Bay bridge, but going all the way to the bank was unusual.

"Yes, my dear." He flashed his gold tooth in a smile. "The whole way."

Emily looked at her parents' faces and knew that she was right. Her bicycle had to be at the bank.

But it wasn't a bicycle that awaited her.

"Here you are, Emily," Father said. "Your very own passbook. This is your account number, and you can see that I've started you off with five whole dollars."

Emily managed a smile. She mustn't appear ungrateful. Besides, it was early yet. The bicycle would likely appear at supper, along with her birthday cake and other presents.

"Where's your bicycle?" Alice asked when Emily arrived at school. "You said you were getting one for your birthday."

"It's coming later," she said.

"That's what you said at Christmas," Tom pointed out. "And you still haven't got it."

"You're not really getting a bicycle at all, are you?" George said. "You're just putting on airs. Father says they're very dear. But even so, I'm sure to get one this summer."

Emily tossed her head. "Well, I'm sure to get one this afternoon."

After school she searched her yard, the wood-shed, and the verandah. A search inside, from attic to cellar, yielded nothing. But the day was far from over.

After supper Hing brought out the birthday cake. Emily closed her eyes, made the same wish she'd been making all year, and blew out the candles. Then Mother brought in her presents. A blue velvet dress. An album for photographs. And something rolled up in brown paper and tied with string.

"Open it, Em!" Jane squirmed with excitement as Emily unrolled the paper. "It's your wish come true."

When Emily saw Jane's gift, her eyes brimmed with tears. It was a drawing of a bicycle, every detail perfect, right down to the bell on the handlebars. Beside it was a smiling little girl meant to be Emily.

"I sketched it in my art class before Christmas," Jane said. "Do you like it?"

"I love it, Jane. I'll hang it in our room straight away." She gave her a hug, then ran upstairs so Jane wouldn't see her crying.

A short time later, Father came in. He patted Emily's shoulder, then took the drawing and tacked it above the bed.

"I know you had your heart set on a real bicycle," he said. "But do you remember our New Year's party, and how we had fewer guests than usual? And how we didn't have a turkey? Well, the fact is, money is rather tight at the moment. As soon as things get better, I promise you'll have your bicycle."

Emily sniffed sadly. "Even if I'm very old, like sixteen?"

"Even if you're a grouchity old thing like me."

"You're not all that grouchity, Father."

He smiled, then reached for his handkerchief and wiped away her tears. "You know, Hing tells me that in a few days it's Chinese New Year. Would you like to go to Chinatown and see the celebration?"

"Oh, yes!" She grinned. "And since it's a new year, you'll have to polish your gold tooth."

"That's my girl! Now, let's go down and finish your cake."

Before going downstairs, Emily patted her bicycle picture and made a wish for better times.

At breakfast on the morning of Chinese New Year, Hing gave Emily two red scrolls decorated with tiny mirrors, paper flowers, and multicoloured tassels. "Hang on bedposts. Keep away bad spirits. Good luck for three little girls, all year. This year," he went on, "is Year of Monkey."

"In China, does every year have a different animal?" Emily wondered.

"Oh, yes. And every animal means different character. You same as my girl, born in Year of

Dog. And Dog Year people . . . oh, my. Can be selfish. Very stubborn. But also, Dog Year people know what is right and fair." He gave her a warm smile.

"Hing," Father said, "in honour of your New Year, you may leave at noon today. And take the whole day off tomorrow."

"Thank you." Hing clasped his hands and bowed. "If I may . . . I take Em-ry to Chinese theatre tomorrow?"

"Oh, Father!" Emily exclaimed. "Please say yes!"

Her parents exchanged glances. Then Father said, "Of course. As long as Hing brings you home in time for tea."

Emily hugged herself with excitement. Tomorrow, the theatre. And today, Chinese New Year!

Hundreds of people turned out for the celebration. Chinatown echoed with the clash of cymbals and the bursting of firecrackers. Bright-red banners flew from shop windows. Enormous paper lanterns dangled from balconies and lamp-posts. Wealthy merchants, dressed in their finest silks, offered wine, nuts, and fruit to the visitors who stopped by their shops. Emily's family received one warm welcome after another.

Every merchant gave each of the girls a small red envelope containing a five-cent piece. "*Lai see*," one merchant explained. "Lucky money. The more we give away, the more luck we get. It's a tradition."

Emily thought it was a grand idea. She waved to two Chinese children clutching their *lai see* envelopes and called out, "*Gung hey fat choy!*" The girls covered their mouths and giggled, but their mother returned Emily's greeting.

"What will you do with your lucky money, Em?" Jane asked. "I'm going to buy some new coloured pencils. May I, Father?"

"Certainly."

"I'm going to buy a pony," said Amelia.

"It will have to be a very small pony." Father chuckled. "How about you, Emily?"

"I'll put it in my new bank account. And save it up for a bicycle."

He looked very pleased.

The Chinese theatre was nothing like the posh Victoria Opera House. Even getting there was an adventure. Emily took Hing's hand as they walked through a maze of alleys, along a narrow passage-way, and up a flight of stairs. At the top, they entered a large, dimly lit room filled with benches. One end of the room served as the stage and was set up with the strangest musical instruments Emily had ever seen. Their sounds were even stranger.

The play had already started when Hing and Emily sat down, and she quickly realized that to follow the story, she had to use her imagination. When a chair was placed on the stage, for example, Hing said, "Mountain." Later, when she asked about two chairs, he said, "House." She was astonished to learn that the actors were always men. Even the women's roles were played by men speaking in high-pitched voices.

And the audience! They fell asleep, coughed and snored, chatted to friends. They stretched their legs and walked across the stage. There was even a group of men playing some kind of clicking game in the back. All this while the play was going on. And the actors didn't even mind!

The best part was that the merchants were still handing out lucky money. There weren't many children at the theatre, but those who were there, including Emily, had a growing pile of red envelopes on their laps.

She was surprised when Hing said it was time to go. "It's not over," she said.

"Play goes on and on and on," he explained. "People come and go. Now time for tea."

They left the theatre and walked out into the sunlight. It was cold and clear, a fine February day, bursting with the sound of firecrackers.

"Will your daughter have firecrackers in China?" Emily asked.

Hing smiled. "Oh, yes! Big firecrackers. Lots of noise!"

"And lucky money?"

"Not much money. Village poor. Maybe little bit."

"I could send her some of mine."

"No, no. You keep."

Half and half, Emily decided. As they walked across the James Bay bridge, she pictured Hing's little girl opening the package from Victoria and finding a *lai see* envelope filled with Canadian coins. She wouldn't be able to spend them, so she'd have to save them for when she came here. In the meantime, she'd have extra luck, and so would Emily.

She'd still save *some* of her New Year's money for a bicycle. As for the rest, Father would understand.

She gave a little skip, realizing how lucky she was that *her* father was not off in some distant land. He was just around the corner, waiting for her to come home.

BOOK TWO

Disaster
at the Bridge

CHAPTER N° 1

"Let's race to the top of the hill!" Emily cried. She had been looking forward to this moment all afternoon, and not only for the joy of being outside with her friend Alice. Earlier that day, the principal of her school had told her that she had a good chance of making the school's running team. The incentive made her run even faster.

It wasn't long before she'd outpaced Alice and reached the top of Beacon Hill. From there, it seemed as if she could see the whole world—sea, sky, mountains, rooftops, trees, and the hill stretching below like a lush green carpet sprinkled with blue camas lilies, buttercups, and purple shooting stars.

"You're too fast for me, Em," Alice gasped as she neared the top. "My heart's bursting!"

Emily extended a hand and pulled Alice the rest of the way. "You've made it! Now we can roll back down."

"I'll beat you this time," Alice said. "I'm much better at rolling."

They smoothed out their pinafores, lay on the grass and rolled down the hill, coming to rest in a patch of wildflowers. Laughing, they shook the leaves and blossoms from their hair and began to make spring garlands.

"George is moving away this week," Alice said. "His father bought a new house on the Gorge." Eleven-year-old George Walsh lived in Emily's neighbourhood, next door to Alice. He and his family had arrived not long ago from England, and Mr. Walsh worked with Emily's father at the bank.

"The Gorge?" Emily said wistfully. "They're so lucky. Some of the wealthiest people in Victoria live there. Father says the Gorge Waterway is the most beautiful part of the city."

"Do you know what else?" Alice continued. "I saw the people who bought the Walshes' house. They're moving in next Thursday, just in time for Easter."

"Do they have any boys?" Emily hoped another George wasn't moving next door to Alice. She did like George, and she would miss him, but his mischievous ideas had landed them both in trouble more than once.

"No, just one girl," Alice said. "I saw her yesterday. She's our age, very tall, and pretty. And she was wearing fashionable clothes. I only saw her through my window so I didn't talk to her. But Tom was outside and he told me that when he said hello, she put her nose in the air and ignored him."

"She sounds like a snob," Emily said.

"Maybe, or she might be shy. Or maybe she

didn't like the look of my brother." Alice concentrated on weaving a few more camas lilies into her garland, then said, "Let's play the favourite game. And remember, you're not allowed to think. Just say the first thing that pops into your mind."

"I know the rules," said Emily. "You go first."

"Favourite place?"

"Beacon Hill. Favourite flower?"

"Easter lilies. Favourite food?"

"Hing's lemon tarts. Best friend?"

"You, of course!" Alice said. "Now, what do you want the most in the whole wide world? And don't say a bicycle."

"A bicycle bell."

"Be serious!" Alice laughed and threw a handful of shooting stars at her friend.

"Very well, then," Emily said. "What I want the most is for us to stay best friends forever."

"Me, too," said Alice. "Do you promise?"

"I promise," Emily replied.

They traded garlands to seal the bargain, then

linked arms and strolled through the park, stopping briefly to see the peacocks in their cages. After that, they parted company, Alice to go home, and Emily to meet her father at the James Bay Bridge.

There was a lot of traffic on the bridge—streetcars, horse-drawn hacks and carriages, people riding bicycles or walking. Emily scanned the crowd, hoping she hadn't missed her father by staying too long in the park. At last she spotted him and called out to get his attention.

He looked a little downcast, but his face brightened when he saw her. He smiled broadly, and Emily caught the familiar glint of his gold tooth. "You're early today."

"Good," she said, taking his hand. "I was afraid I might be late. See the flower necklace that Alice made?" She told him about rolling down the hill in the park and asked him about the Walsh family's move. "Would you like to live on the Gorge, Father?"

"Hmm? What's that about George?"

"Not George, Gorge!" She shook his arm impatiently.

"I'm sorry, dear. My mind's wandering."

Emily frowned. It wasn't like Father to be so absent-minded. "What's wrong? Did something happen at the bank?"

"Nothing for you to worry about." He plucked a stray buttercup from her hair. "Tell me about your day. You were saying something about the Gorge? How was school?"

She repeated what she'd already told him, then went on to say that school had been rather dull, except for the races.

"We're going to have running practice twice a week because there's going to be a sports day on the 24th of May, and all the schools in Victoria are taking part. Miss Cameron said that it will actually be on the 25th because the 24th is a

Sunday, but still, that's less than two months away. And Miss Cameron told me I had a good chance of running for South Park School because I won almost every race this morning."

"Well done!"

"George had a good chance too, but now he's going to be moving to another school. Miss Cameron said the races will be on the same day as the regatta, but in the morning, thank goodness! So we won't miss the regatta. And the day after that is the military tattoo. I can't wait until the 24th of May, can you?"

"No, that's one bright light to look forward to."

Only *one* bright light? Emily couldn't help but wonder what was troubling him. Ever since New Year's Day, when she'd heard her father talking to the other grown-ups about "tough times," his comment had gnawed at the back of her mind. What exactly did "tough times" mean? She'd recently overheard a neighbour telling her mother that he'd lost his job as a city worker because the city was hard pressed for money and could keep only a small staff. Then they'd started talking about "tough times" and "depression."

Whenever she asked her parents or their Chinese cook, Hing, about the situation, they told her not to worry. But she couldn't help it. It was one thing not being able to afford fancy new things, but what if "depression" meant something far worse?

She knew that something had happened to Father. All the way home he seemed preoccupied. His voice was quiet and his step wasn't as brisk as usual. And later, at supper, he scarcely said a word.

That night, when Mother came to tuck in the girls, Emily said bluntly, "What's the matter with Father?"

Her mother sighed. "He didn't get a promotion at the bank. He was expecting it, you see, and so he's very disappointed."

"Like when Emily didn't get a bicycle for her birthday?" asked four-year-old Amelia.

"Yes," Mother replied. "But pretty soon he'll feel better."

"Emily didn't."

"She did so!" eight-year-old Jane argued. "Didn't you, Em?"

Emily glanced up at the bicycle picture Jane had given her and nodded. She had felt better, eventually. But she still yearned for a bicycle. Just thinking about it made the knot of disappointment tighten up inside. If that was how Father was feeling, it was no wonder he was distracted. But at least he wasn't ill or dying or moving away. It wasn't the end of the world.

CHAPTER N° 2

A few days later, Emily was curled up in the parlour, attempting to do some needlework, when Hing entered the room.

"Em-ry," he said, pronouncing her name as best he could.

Something in his tone told Emily she had better pay attention. She put down the needlework—the tiny stitches were giving her a headache anyway—and looked up. "What's wrong?"

"No!" Hing said. "Not *long*, not bad. *Good* news. Big change for me, you, family . . ."

He proceeded to explain.

Emily listened. Hing's news was hard to follow, and not only because of the confusing mix of l's for r's and r's for l's. Head tax, loans . . . restaurant, China . . . wife and sons and daughter . . . She couldn't take it all in, but one thing was clear. Hing was leaving.

"Why?" Her voice quavered. "I thought you liked it here. Oh, Hing, you *can't* go!"

"Today, last day of March," he said. "I give notice. Go two months, end of May. Em-ry . . . listen. Want own family here. And business. Friend go back to China, want to sell restaurant in Chinatown. I borrow money from Chinese merchant, buy restaurant. Pay head tax for wife and children. They come, work in restaurant. You come, eat in restaurant. Everybody happy."

"I'm not!" She burst into tears, flung the needlework onto the floor and ran outside, just as her father was coming up the path.

"Father, can't we persuade him to stay?" she cried.

"Don't I even get a hello?" he said. "Persuade who to stay?"

"Hing! He just told me he's leaving."

"Oh, dear. I'm sorry I didn't tell you, but with everything else . . . We'll miss him, of course, but it's a fine opportunity. Imagine, his own restaurant! Good for him."

"It's *not* good! What'll I do?" Hing was more than just a servant to Emily, he was a friend, a friend she'd known all her life. She couldn't imagine the house without him.

"Emily." Father took her hands and crouched down in front of her. "The world does not revolve around you or me or any of us, for that matter. If Hing has the chance to get ahead, I say good for him. And so must you."

That night, as Emily lay in bed, she thought about Hing and his family. Her mood brightened as she pictured their reunion. He hadn't seen them in ten years. And how happy he would be to meet his daughter, Mei Yuk, for the first time. Emily looked forward to meeting her too, especially since they were both born in the Year of the Dog. They were practically sisters! And maybe they could be good friends.

The next day, Emily hurried home from school to write Mei Yuk a letter. She gathered the necessary materials, dipped her brush in the thick, black ink, then bent over a sheet of paper, her face scrunched in concentration. Carefully, as Hing had taught her, she made the characters for "Mei" and "Yuk."

She had been practising calligraphy for weeks, other characters, too—like the ones for dragon and dog, mother and father. She didn't know enough for a whole letter, but at least she could begin with Mei Yuk's name.

Hing had told her that Mei Yuk meant

"Beautiful Jade." She wished her name meant something beautiful. Her mother had told her that Emily meant "industrious." Of all the dreary meanings for a name. Why couldn't it mean "swift" or "fast as lightning"?

Emily looked up as Hing entered the room and proudly showed him her calligraphy.

"Good!" He beamed. "Practice make perfect."

"I hope she writes back this time," Emily said. She had written to Mei Yuk during Chinese New Year and had enclosed a *lai see* envelope containing some lucky money, a New Year's gift. But she had never received a reply.

"Mail slow," Hing said. "Boat to Canton, China, take weeks. Then find village, take many days. Maybe letters pass in ocean. Em-ry go east, Mei Yuk go west!"

Emily smiled at the thought, then picked up a pencil and continued her letter.

Victoria, B.C.
Wednesday, April 1, 1896

Dear Mei Yuk (Beautiful Jade),
　How are you? I hope you are fine.

　In case you did not receive the letter I wrote in February, my name is Emily and your father is our cook. He told me that you are coming to live in Victoria. I hope you will go to South Park School and be in my class. I will help you learn English. Alice will help, too. She is my best friend.

　Would you like to be called by your Chinese name or by your English name? Both names are very beautiful.

　I hope someone in your village will read my letter to you.

　I hope we will be friends.

Yours truly,
Emily Murdoch

CHAPTER N.º 3

A frog, a log, and a dog . . . Emily tightened her grip on her pen and tried to concentrate on the day's lesson. But goodness, it was difficult. Especially on such a warm April day.

She leaned on her desk, chin in hand, and gazed out the window. She could hear the song of a red-winged blackbird and, every so often, the shrill cry of a peacock. As soon as school was out, she'd go to the park and feed the ducks. Maybe Alice would come . . . unless she was too busy with that *new* girl.

She groaned silently. The memory of her first meeting with Florence Featherby-Jones still rankled. It had taken place after church on Easter Sunday, when the whole neighbourhood had gathered in Beacon Hill Park for an Easter celebration.

The first event was an egg-rolling contest. Each child was given a coloured, hard-boiled egg and told to throw it down the hill. The one whose egg went the farthest got the prize.

Florence was put out because her egg didn't win. She was about to leave in a sulk when the Easter egg hunt was announced. There were eggs hidden everywhere—jelly eggs, cream eggs, hard-boiled eggs, and a few specially decorated chocolate eggs. Emily had just stumbled upon one of the chocolate eggs when Florence pushed her out of the way and grabbed it for herself.

And later, the way Florence had gone on about London, where she used to live, and the parties she'd attended at Buckingham Palace—only one, according to her mother—you'd have thought she was in line for the throne.

"Emily!"

Miss Lorimer's voice made her jump.

"Are you paying attention?"

"Yes, Miss."

"Well, then, sit *squarely* facing your desk. And mind how you're holding your pen. No wonder your writing is sloppy."

Florence snickered across the aisle.

"Hold your pen lightly," Miss Lorimer continued. "That's it, between the end of the thumb and the first two fingers."

Emily rolled her eyes but did as she was told. She hated her pen. It was long and straight and jumped out of her hand if she didn't keep a firm grip. And the metal nib made a sound more grating than the scrape of chalk on the blackboard.

A frog, a log, and a dog . . .

Six lines in her copybook. Six frogs, six logs, six dogs . . . What was the frog doing on the log? Who owned the dog? Was the log on the beach? Or near a bog? In the fog? She stifled a giggle.

She had almost finished when Florence leaned across the aisle and knocked over her inkwell.

"Oh, no!" Emily cried. She leapt up and grabbed her copybook, then opened the lid of her desk. A stream of ink was flowing through the crack, over her papers, pencils, copybooks, everything.

"I'm sorry," Florence said. She took a cloth from her desk and began to wipe up. "It was an accident. I only wanted to borrow your extra nib."

When the worst of the mess was cleaned up, Emily thanked Florence for helping, but she wondered if it really had been an accident. Florence hadn't been pleased when her mother had made her give Emily the chocolate Easter egg. Four days had gone by, but perhaps she was still holding a grudge.

As it turned out, Alice couldn't feed the ducks after school because she'd promised to go to Florence's house. Emily was invited to join them, but it wasn't long before she was wishing she'd gone to the park by herself.

"You know, Emily," Florence said as they were walking along, "your face is very red. It looks as though you wash it with strawberry juice. Don't you want your skin to be white? I do. That's why I'm a vegetarian. I eat no meat whatsoever."

Emily and Alice raised their eyebrows. "What do you eat?" Emily asked. "Don't you get hungry?"

"No," Florence replied. "For breakfast I eat oatmeal and oranges. For dinner I might have fruit and nuts, or cauliflower croquettes and stewed vegetables. And I drink fruit tea, preferably quince."

Alice pulled a face. "It sounds dreadful."

"My mother considers that caring for one's health and complexion is a duty," said Florence. Her tone clearly implied that *some* girls' mothers were failing in their duty. "You can improve your appearance, Emily. You too, Alice."

"There's nothing wrong with Alice's appearance," Emily said loyally.

"Or Emily's," said Alice.

"There's always room for improvement," Florence said. "But you have to abstain from bread and butter and sweets."

"I'd never give up sweets," said Emily. "And what about you and the Easter eggs? You weren't abstaining then."

"That was Easter," Florence said, as if that explained everything.

"What should we drink?" Alice wondered. "Besides quince tea."

"A glass of clear water every day before breakfast. Or lemonade."

"It's not too late, is it?" said Alice. "If we want to be as pretty as you?"

"Alice!" Emily's mouth dropped. Surely her friend wasn't serious.

"It's never too late." Florence smiled. "You know, when I was in London . . ."

By the time they'd reached Florence's house,

Emily had had enough. She made her excuses and hurried home, then looked in the mirror to see if Florence was right. Of course, her face turned red when she ran, or when she was embarrassed, but not all the time. As for strawberry juice? The nerve! She wished she could have told Florence how to improve her big teeth and gummy smile. Or how to get rid of her silly dimples.

She had to admit that the new girl was clever, though. She got perfect scores in spelling and almost perfect scores in arithmetic. Her penmanship was praised to the skies. And when the teacher asked a question, Florence always knew the answer.

Emily knew the answers, too—most of them, anyway—but the teacher always seemed to call on Florence.

"She thinks she knows everything," Emily complained to Alice one day. It was a Saturday, and they were sitting on top of Beacon Hill making daisy chains. "She's such a snob. She looks down on us, you know. I heard her say she was glad *she* wasn't born in the colonies. Doesn't she know Canada isn't a colony any more? And she says we don't speak proper English."

Alice gave a loud sigh. "Oh, Em! Don't let it bother you. I like Florence. She's a bit spoiled—"

"More than a bit!"

"But she tells funny stories and makes me laugh."

"They're not true."

"I know, but what diffcrence does it make?" She placed her daisy chain on Emily's head. "This is your crown. Because you're still the best runner."

"Do you really think so?"

"Of course! Now let's play. Favourite subject?"

"Calisthenics. Favourite colour?"

"Blue. Favourite boy?"

"George."

"George?" Alice shrieked.

Emily clapped a hand to her mouth. "No! I

didn't mean George, I meant Father! What was I thinking?"

"Favourite candy?"

"Jawbreakers. Best friend?"

"Quince tea!" Alice hooted with laughter.

"What?"

"I'm joking, silly. You're my best friend."

Emily smiled, but for the first time ever, she felt a twinge of doubt.

CHAPTER N⁰ 4

"Warm-ups first!" Miss Cameron said to the assembled group. "Ten minutes jogging around the field."

Florence raised her hand. "Excuse me, Miss Cameron. I don't see the need for warm-ups. We never did them in London."

"But you're not in London now," Miss Cameron said, "and we don't want you to run the risk of pulling a muscle. Follow Emily's example. She knows the value of a good warm-up."

Emily set off at a light jog, pleased that Miss

Cameron, the principal, had singled her out.

There were twenty girls and boys in all. Today's session was to determine which pupils would make the final cut and compete in the 24th of May races, now four weeks away.

As they jogged around the field, Emily noticed Alice watching from the sidelines. "Good luck, Em!" she called out. "You too, Florence! I hope you both make the team!"

Emily weighed her chances. She was the youngest in the group, but one of the fastest sprinters. Florence was fast too, but why wouldn't she be? She was perfect at everything.

Before Florence arrived, there was no question of Emily not making the team. But now, if Miss Cameron had to choose between them . . .

Stop it! she scolded herself. *There's nothing you can do but try your best.*

It wasn't as though she hadn't been practising. Hing never had to beat the dinner gong at noon, because she was making it home in less than three minutes. Mother said she was so fast on her feet that she'd never need a bicycle.

She hadn't missed a single after-school practice and, in their daily calisthenics class, she worked harder than anyone. She'd learned to run on the balls of her feet and to lift her knees high to get longer strides. She'd also learned that the faster she swung her arms, the faster her legs would move. Her legs were short—much shorter than Florence's—but they were strong. Most important, she'd learned to ignore the runners on either side, because any distraction—a glance or even a passing thought—could cost precious time.

At the sound of Miss Cameron's whistle, she jogged back to the starting line. Stretching was the next part of the warm up and, for once, Florence didn't feel the need to tell everyone how it was done in London.

Then it was time for the races. First, the 220-yard dash. Emily started fast, eased up a little, then drove for the tape at the end and came in fourth.

Florence was first. "You should have started your final burst a bit sooner," she told Emily.

"That's what I did."

There were a few races for the boys, and then for the older pupils. Finally it was time for Emily's favourite—the 100-yard dash.

"On your marks . . . Get set . . . GO!"

Emily's start was explosive. She flew down the track, knees high, arms pumping at her sides, her concentration focused on a point beyond the tape—and she made it first across the finish line.

Florence was a close second.

After everyone had caught their breath, Miss Cameron made her announcement. Emily waited anxiously as, one by one, the names were called out.

". . . Florence Featherby-Jones . . . and last but not least—usually first, come to think of it," Miss Cameron quipped, "Emily Murdoch."

"Hurray!" Alice ran over and gave each girl a hug, then invited them to her house to play hopscotch.

Emily said she couldn't because of her chores, but it was only an excuse. She hated playing games with Florence. If Florence won, she gloated, and if she lost, she sulked.

All the same, Emily felt left out as she watched the two girls link arms and walk off together. It made her realize that staying friends with Alice would mean making friends with Florence. She vowed to try.

Emily was doing her best to get along with Florence and felt that she was succeeding quite admirably—until the day Florence came to school with a bicycle.

Emily had never seen such a beautiful bicycle. It was a Raleigh, shipped all the way from England, with silvery spokes and chain, a red enamel finish, and a black leather saddle. It even had a brass kerosene lamp and a double-stroke bell with a pure, clear sound.

"You may think the colour is red," Florence told

her admiring classmates, "but it's not. It's vermilion."

"Vermilion," Emily murmured. Everything about the bicycle was perfect, even the name of the colour.

At lunchtime, Florence made a surprising offer. "Would anyone like to ride it?"

"Me! I would!" Everyone was shouting at once. "Please, Florence! Pick me!"

"Pick Emily!" said Alice. "She's longing for a bicycle. And she knows how to ride one."

Emily blushed. Where had Alice got that idea? She'd never actually ridden a bicycle. But it couldn't be that difficult, could it?

"Come on, then." Florence held the bicycle steady as Emily climbed on. "I'll push until we're out of the schoolyard."

Emily smiled. It felt wonderful.

Once they were on the street, Florence said, "Don't look down or you might lose your balance."

"She knows that," said Alice.

"The seat's a bit high," Emily said. "I can hardly reach the pedals."

Florence didn't seem to hear. She gave her a shove and stepped back.

"Wait!" Emily cried. "Don't let go, I'm not—"

"Keep pedalling!"

Emily tried. Before she knew it, the bicycle had hit a slope and was rapidly gaining speed.

"Brakes! Put on the brakes!"

Brakes? Where were the brakes? Emily had no idea how to stop a bicycle.

Everyone was running and yelling.

"Backwards! Pedal backwards!"

"Look out!"

"You're going to crash!"

In desperation, Emily pushed the top pedal backwards. The bicycle slammed to a stop. Over she went, in a flurry of skirts and spinning wheels, and landed in the bushes beside the road.

Tears stung her eyes. Her hands were grazed, she'd bitten her lip, and her bones ached from head to toe.

Florence was furious. "You crashed my bicycle! Don't you know they're coaster brakes? You're not meant to *jam* them!"

"Are you all right, Em?" Alice knelt down and offered Emily her handkerchief.

"I should never have let you ride it," Florence continued. "You said you knew how!"

Emily didn't bother to correct her. She just wiped her eyes with Alice's handkerchief and limped away with as much dignity as she could manage.

Back at the school, she went into the water closet, cleaned herself up, and cried.

"Emily?" It was Alice at the door. "Miss Cameron's about to ring the bell. You'd better hurry."

"Go away."

"Florence said she was sorry."

"I don't believe you. She hates me and I hate her. She's nothing but a—a *depression*." It wasn't the right word, but it summed up her feelings, as well

as all the things that had been going wrong.

On the way to her classroom, Emily was stopped by Miss Cameron, who took one look at her scrapes and promptly led her to the medicine chest. "Can't have you injured for the 24th, can we?" she said. "There! A little witch hazel will do the trick." She dabbed the soothing lotion on Emily's hands and lip and asked what had happened.

"I was trying to ride Florence's bicycle," Emily said.

"Good for you! The only way to learn is by doing."

"But I didn't learn. I fell off."

"Never mind. Some people learn right away and others take longer. A few more lessons and you'll be on your way. And I promise you, once you learn how, you'll never forget. Now . . . feeling better?"

Emily nodded. Not that she'd ever have another lesson. Or a bicycle.

By the time she returned to her classroom, everyone was working on the spelling lesson. Last week, the lesson had been "What a Boy or Girl Should Be." This week, it was the opposite. Emily took out her copybook. With a shaky hand, still smarting from her fall, she wrote the heading and copied the words from the blackboard.

What a Boy or Girl Should *Not* Be:

> bad
>
> mean
>
> proud
>
> lazy
>
> sulky
>
> saucy
>
> stingy

The list went on: selfish, fretful, profane, vicious, heedless, impolite, deceitful, dishonest, cowardly, quarrelsome.

As far as Emily was concerned, every word described Florence.

CHAPTER N.º 5

Emily had seldom known an afternoon to pass so slowly. She tried to concentrate on her lessons, but all she could think about was the special tea she was having with Alice. They'd arranged it days ago, as soon as Emily had heard that her Friday practice was cancelled. It would be like old times, just the two of them, and this time, she would not mention Florence.

Finally the afternoon came to an end. Emily was gathering up her things, eagerly planning what they might do after tea, when she saw Alice and Florence leaving the cloakroom, arm in arm.

"Alice, wait!" she called. "Aren't you coming home with me? It's our tea, remember?"

Alice's face dropped. "Oh, no! I'm sorry, Em. I completely forgot. And yesterday I promised Florence . . ." She looked from one to the other, clearly embarrassed. "We were going to play her new board game, but now she's going to teach me to ride her bicycle." She whispered something in Florence's ear and Florence, after glancing at Emily, nodded grudgingly.

"You can come too," said Alice.

"No, I can't. I have to be home for tea."

"Well, then, come after tea. That's all right, isn't it, Florence?"

Mean, sulky Florence said nothing.

When Emily got home she found the tea laid out in the parlour, with settings for two and a plate of Hing's special lemon tarts. She took one look and burst into tears.

"Emily!" Her mother and sisters rushed into the room, followed by an anxious Hing. "What's wrong?" Mother said. "Where's Alice?"

"She went off with Florence!" Emily sobbed. "And now I don't have any friends."

"You have us," Jane said. "We'll stay for tea."

Emily managed a smile. Before long, another two places were laid.

"You can invite Alice another time," Mother said. "I'm sure she didn't forget on purpose."

"You stop worry," Hing said. "Think of race. Only two week away. I make special dish—rice for energy, and chicken—make you run fast, stay strong."

Emily sniffed. "Will it make Alice and Florence like me?"

"Ha!" Hing snorted. "They don't like you, they big loser. You winner. You born Year of Dog, remember? Like . . ." He thought for a moment. "Greyhound! Very fast."

Amelia giggled. "Emily's a greyhound!"

"Florence is a big bad wolfhound," said Jane.

"What am I?" Amelia wanted to know.

"You Pekingese!" Hing said, and everyone laughed.

After tea, Emily set off for the bridge as usual to wait for her father. On the way, she met Alice.

"I was coming to your house," Alice said. "Can I walk with you?"

"Where's your new friend?" Emily said bitterly.

"You could have come with us."

"No, I couldn't. Hing had everything ready for tea, and Florence didn't want me. And what would I have done? Stood around and watched while you rode her bicycle? I bet she didn't make *you* fall."

"No," Alice admitted. "Anyway, we spent most

of the time playing games. You should have come over after tea. She wants to be friends, you know."

"No, she doesn't. She doesn't even like me— and I know why. It's because I don't fawn all over her the way you do."

Alice stopped in her tracks. "I don't *fawn*."

"Yes, you do." Emily wished she could take back the words but it was too late. Before she could stop herself, she blundered on. " 'Oh, Florence,' " she mimicked, " 'you have such *pretty* hair. Your clothes are so *stylish*. You're so *clever*. You're such a good runner . . .' "

"I never said that."

"It's pathetic."

"Well, I like her, Emily. So there! And if you don't want to play with us, you can play by yourself." With that, she stormed away.

Emily watched her go, sick at heart. Alice had come to make amends and instead of being happy and grateful, she'd behaved in a rude, spiteful, despicable way. She was everything a friend should *not* be.

On Friday evening, after a whole week of being ignored by Alice, Emily sat down with paper and pencil and wrote Hing's daughter a letter. At least she had Mei Yuk for a friend.

Friday, May 15, 1896

Dear Mei Yuk,

I am sorry for not writing your name in calligraphy, but I am too upset to concentrate. Last week I had a fight with my best friend, Alice. I said mean things because I am jealous. Florence is pretty and clever and stylish. She is also a very fast runner, and she has a bicycle, and now she has Alice for her friend.

I promise that from now on I will try to be what a friend should be: kind, brave, noble, polite, honest, thoughtful, and loving. I will also be understanding, if you want to play with someone else sometimes.

Yours truly,

Emily Murdoch

Emily was reading over the words when it dawned on her—the letter should really go to Alice! Poor Mei Yuk would be so confused by such an outpouring of feelings that she might never want to hear from Emily again, let alone meet her. She erased Mei Yuk's name and wrote "Alice." Then, before she could change her mind, she put the letter in an envelope and ran outside to drop it in the letter box.

CHAPTER N.º 6

"Why so quiet, Em? Oh, I know!" Jane grinned. "You're excited about seeing George!"

Emily rolled her eyes and refused to rise to Jane's bait. She had been gazing out the streetcar window, thinking about her letter to Alice. It would have been collected that morning and taken to the post office. There was no delivery tomorrow, being Sunday, but Alice might have the letter as early as Monday.

Her thoughts now turned to George. His parents had invited the Murdochs to their new house on the Gorge for a pre-holiday picnic and, although Emily was looking forward to the picnic, she had mixed feelings about George. It was almost two months since she'd last seen him, and she couldn't help but wonder how he might behave. Endless bragging, no doubt. And teasing whenever he got the chance. Maybe he'd dare her to do something reckless—like jump into the freezing waters of the Gorge, or spy on the neighbours. She began to brace herself for what might be a long and unpleasant afternoon.

She needn't have worried. George appeared pleased to see her and her family and led them all out to the garden for a picnic feast. Cold roast beef, veal-and-ham pies, sliced tomatoes, bread-and-butter sandwiches, stuffed eggs, pickles and olives, cake and lemonade!

While they were eating, Emily gave George the news about his former school and classmates, and told him that she'd made the running team.

George grinned. "Then you'll be competing

against me in the 100-yard dash," he said. "Think you've got a chance?"

"I've beaten you before," Emily said. "Remember all those times at Beacon Hill? And that was running uphill!"

"Who else is on the team?"

"Florence, the girl who moved into your old house. She's really fast and she hates to lose." She was about to say more when George leapt up and shouted, "Roger!"

Emily turned and saw an older version of George walking towards them, dressed in a Royal Navy uniform.

"This is my brother, Roger," George said proudly. "He's taking part in the regatta on Monday and in the pageant on Tuesday, in the sham battle." He introduced everyone and, after a short time, the two wandered off together.

"What's a 'jam battle'?" Amelia asked.

"It's *sham*," said Emily. "It's pretend."

"But what does it mean?"

Emily swallowed her last bit of cake, then

jumped up and began to march. "I remember from last year, so I'll show you. You too, Jane. Come on, we'll play pageant. Hup, two, three, four! Order Arms! Shoulder Arms! Here come the Bluejackets!"

"What's Bluejackets?" asked Amelia.

"The Royal Navy, like Roger. Hup, two, three, four. Now, here come the Marines. And here's the Fifth Regiment. Hup, two, three—eyes front, Amelia. Jane, stop laughing. *Jane!*"

"I can't help it! Look at George!"

Emily turned and caught George imitating her behind her back. She blushed and was about to run off when Roger said, "Don't pay any attention to George, Emily. You make a fine officer."

His words made her blush even harder.

Amelia tugged on his sleeve. "Why don't you play too?"

"Amelia!" Emily glared at her sister. "He's a grown-up."

"We'll all play," Roger said. "Even George. He's never seen Victoria's famous pageant, and I've been rehearsing all week. File in, George."

After a few more rounds of marching, Jane asked Roger to tell them about the pageant.

"It's very thrilling," he explained. "First, there's a march past the Admiral with salutes and cannon fire. Then there are physical drills with sword-bayonets. Then the 5th Regiment mounts and dismounts the nine-pounders— those are the big guns—and after all that, there's the sham battle."

"And it's just pretend," said Amelia.

"Oh, yes. No one gets hurt. The Bluejackets try to reach the fort while the artillery tries to keep them away. Attack and defend, like in a real battle."

"But it's only pretend."

"Amelia!" Jane and Emily groaned.

Roger patted Amelia's head. "You are a worry-wart, aren't you?"

"No, Emily's the worrywart. That's what Father says."

"Worrywart!" George teased.

"I am not!" Emily protested, even though she knew it was true.

"It's all good fun," Roger went on, "but you have to keep well off the parade ground for your own safety. And so you won't interfere with the battle."

"And it's just pretend," said Amelia.

"Amelia!"

"Safe as houses!" Roger laughed. "Nevertheless, I expect to hear all of you cheering loudly for the Bluejackets on Tuesday. Can we count on you?"

Emily and Jane nodded vigorously, and Amelia piped up, "Can we practise now? Hurrah for the Bluejackets!"

"Hurrah for the Bluejackets," they all shouted, and they played pageant until it was time to go home.

CHAPTER N° 7

美玉

The rain was falling in sheets and the wind was blowing a gale. All day long Emily worried about the weather. Only two days until Sunday, the 24th of May, and three days until the start of the holiday. What if the weather didn't change? What if the school sports were cancelled? Or the regatta?

By the time she got home she was tired of worrying, and pushed the "what ifs" out of her mind. It could rain all it liked, at least until Monday. Now she had something else to think about.

She dipped her brush in the ink and wrote Mei Yuk's name. The calligraphy made her smile. Alice had received her letter on Tuesday afternoon and had come right over to Emily's house. After giving Emily a hug and saying she was sorry too, she'd asked, "What's calligraphy? It's the only part of your letter I didn't understand." Emily had promised to teach Alice what little calligraphy she knew.

Victoria, B.C.
Friday, May 22, 1896

Dear Mei Yuk,

How are you? I am feeling much better than I did a few days ago. I had a terrible fight with my best friend, Alice, but we both apologized and made up. I told her about the letters I'm writing to you, and she says she hopes that we can all be friends.

In three days I will be running in some races. Hing made me a special soup. He said it was made with chicken feet, because chickens run fast, but I think he was joking (about the feet). He is a very good cook and his new restaurant is going to be very nice. He said I could help him think of a name, but it has to be a lucky name. I think he is lucky already because soon he will see his whole family.

After the races there is a regatta with lots of boats. We are going in a boat parade at night and Hing gave me a Chinese lantern especially for the occasion.

Please write back to me.

Yours truly,
Emily Murdoch

She sighed, saddened by the thought of Hing. He was leaving at the end of May, only one week away. It would be different at home without him, and she was glad she had the holiday to take her mind off his leaving. He'd told her that he was glad too, because he would miss her very much.

Earlier that week, her family had gone to Chinatown to see his restaurant. It was in a brick building near Fan Tan Alley, very small, but nicely decorated with lanterns and pictures of dragons.

Remembering this, she suddenly had an idea. She reached for a new sheet of paper and eagerly began to apply the brush strokes.

By Sunday night, the worst of the rain was over. Emily lay in bed, too excited to sleep, and said a few extra prayers for a fine, sunny day on Monday. She also said a prayer of thanks that she and Alice were friends once more.

"Em?" Jane whispered. "Are you awake?"

"Yes," Emily whispered back.

"I hope you win tomorrow. I hope you win every single race."

CHAPTER № 8

The moment had arrived. Emily stood at the starting line, her heart pounding. She'd won the 220-yard dash, beating Florence by a nose. Now it was time for the final event and the greatest challenge—the 100-yard dash.

The stands were packed. In spite of the cool, cloudy weather, people from all over Victoria had turned out to watch the public school sports at Beacon Hill. Emily's whole family was there, even Hing. How proud they would be if she could take home the blue ribbon for this race!

"On your marks!" the starter boomed.

Emily squatted down and positioned her hands behind the line. She gazed at the track in front of her, took a few deep breaths and tried to relax.

"Get set!"

She gathered herself for the start. Crouched and ready, she waited for the gun.

BANG!

She shoved off hard and thrust forward, aiming herself straight down the track with a smooth and rhythmic stride. Then, without thinking, she glanced over her shoulder.

Florence was gaining on her.

Come on, Em! She pushed herself harder, pumped her arms, and drove her legs to maintain her speed. Almost there—

Suddenly, she stumbled. She fought to keep from falling, but before she knew it she was on the ground.

She caught her breath and struggled to her feet. Tears welled up, from hurt pride as much as from sore knees. She could see from the crowds milling about that the race was over, but she hadn't finished. After brushing away the tears, she ran her best across the finish line.

Friends and family gathered around to make sure she was all right.

"What happened?" Alice said. "You've never fallen before."

"I'm fine," Emily assured everyone. "I don't know what happened. One minute I was up and the next minute . . ." She smiled sadly. "Who won?"

"George came in second," Jane said, "and another boy from Victoria West came third. Florence came first."

"Where is Florence?" Emily looked around but Florence was nowhere to be seen.

"She won," George said, "but it wasn't an accident when you stumbled. I saw her push you with her elbow. She cheated!"

"No!" Alice said. "She wouldn't dare!"

"Well, she did. I told the teachers. They asked her and she denied it. But where is she now?

Probably gone off with a guilty conscience."

"I'll find out," Alice said.

Emily swallowed hard. Had she been pushed? The slightest nudge would have set her off balance. And Florence had been so close. What should she do? Confront Florence directly? Her reaction would surely reveal something.

Moments later, when she saw Florence leaving the field with her parents, she lost her nerve. All she could say was, "Congratulations."

Florence's face turned crimson. When she turned away without speaking, and with no sign of her usual haughtiness, Emily was convinced that George was right.

"You've done a fine job today," Father said as they were walking home. "And crossing that finish line, even though the race was over—what spunk!" He gave her a hug. "Don't be sad. There'll be plenty of other races."

"But Florence pushed me. It wasn't fair."

"It was mean," Jane said. "Something bad should happen to her."

Emily agreed.

"Now, girls," Mother said. "It may well have been an accident. I think we should set the matter aside and not let it spoil our day. What do you say, Emily?"

"I'll try," she said.

By noon, when the royal salute was fired to announce the beginning of the regatta, she had almost put it out of her mind.

"Everything that floats is here!" Emily exclaimed as she and her sisters ran down to the shore. Father and Mother followed with rugs, cushions, and picnic baskets, and George and his parents weren't far behind. Before long, two cloths were spread out on the lawn and everyone was tucking into their picnic.

The Murdochs had once again been invited to the Walshes' home, this time to watch the regatta.

Mr. Walsh had even offered his rowboat for their return trip.

All thoughts of the race were put aside as Emily munched on a cold chicken leg and viewed the scene. The two barges at the head of the course were already filling up with regatta officials, and overhead, stretching from shore to shore, a line of colourful pennants snapped in the breeze.

On neighbouring lawns and along the wooded banks of the Gorge, hundreds of people were laying out their picnic lunches. Small fires were being built to boil water for tea, and hammocks were strung between trees. Some youngsters were wading into the water for their first swim of the year, although it was bitingly cold. Emily had not ventured more than a toe.

Decked with flags and streamers, the boats sailed up the Gorge, from the Inner Harbour, under the Point Ellice Bridge, and on to the head of the course—punts, rowboats, dinghies, sailboats, dugout canoes, and yachts. Many people who didn't have their own boats were coming by barge, towed by a steam-powered launch.

Even before the races started there was entertainment on the waterway. Lightweight sculls crashed into heavier boats, paddlers got drenched by the wash of the barges, and some rowboats were so overloaded they looked as if they might sink.

By the time Emily was finishing her strawberries and cream, the cutters and galleys of the Royal Navy were heading up to the starting point. Emily recognized Roger among the crew and called out a hearty greeting.

Just then, the sound of a bugle announced the first event—the single-paddle canoe race. The contestants lined up at the starting point, the cannon roared, and off they went, paddling feverishly to Point Ellice Bridge and back.

One race after another—sculls, cutters, canoes, four oars, ten oars, twelve oars—Emily could scarcely keep track.

She cheered the loudest for the Royal Navy. They had the heaviest boats and the longest course, two and a half miles, all the way from the starter's barge and around Deadman's Island.

Next to the Royal Navy contests, her favourite events were the Indian races. The Indians paddled forty-foot war canoes, with thirteen paddlers going like fury and the canoes so close together there was hardly any clear water between them. The Indian women, in their turn, paddled as furiously as the men.

The regatta was so thrilling, Emily had all but forgotten the incident with Florence—until Jane brought it up. They were watching a canoe race when one of the paddlers broke a blade and the others, instead of dashing on, stopped to throw him a spare. When they started a second time, another contestant fell into the water. The man who'd broken his paddle jumped in and helped him get back into the canoe.

"That's what Florence should have done when you fell," Jane said. "She should have stopped and helped you up, like a good sport. That's what you would have done if she'd fallen, isn't it, Em?"

Emily hesitated. She wanted to think that she would have been a good sport and done the right thing. But with Florence . . .

Fortunately, the start of the greasy-pole contest kept her from pursuing the matter. To many, it was the highlight of the afternoon. Eight sailors had lined up for the chance to win the prize—a few silver dollars and a little black pig hanging in a bag at the end of a long, slippery pole that stretched out over the water. As one sailor after another received a dunking, Emily's hopes soared for the pig.

Then the last sailor went out on the pole. Step by step, tottering here, lunging there, but still keeping his balance, he reached the end. To the cheers of the crowd, he removed the bag from the pole and belly-flopped into the water, his squealing prize in hand.

Daylight faded quickly after the final event, but the best part was yet to come—the illuminated boat parade.

The steam launch was ready and waiting. On its return to the Inner Harbour, it was towing not only the barge of holiday-makers but also all the boats taking part in the parade. One by one, the boaters arranged their crafts behind the barge.

At the sound of a gunshot, hundreds of paper lanterns hanging from the barge were lit. Lamps and torches glowed from every boat. Father lit Emily's Chinese lantern and gave it to her to hold.

Slowly and silently the procession moved over the water. Lanterns shone on both sides of the Gorge, from bridges, porches, and verandahs. A huge bonfire burned on Deadman's Island. The water gleamed with reflected light.

"It's like magic," Emily whispered. She looked up in awe as they approached the Point Ellice Bridge, where hundreds of people stood with blazing torches. As the floating pageant drifted beneath the bridge, the crowd began to sing "God Save the Queen."

Emily sang with all her heart. "Send Her victorious, happy and glorious . . ."

She hugged the glorious feeling all the way home.

"Is the whole world taking the streetcar?"
Emily frowned, worried that there might not be
enough room for everyone. The streets were
packed with people, all heading towards the main
streetcar station to get on a car for Esquimalt. No
one wanted to miss the military tattoo.

"Don't fret," Father said. "Every car available
has been pressed into service. There'll be plenty
of room."

Emily wasn't convinced. When they finally
reached the station she saw that two cars were

already filling up with passengers. "Are you sure there's space for all of us?"

"It might be a squeeze," Father admitted. "Stay close and we'll see."

He was about to usher the family onto Car 6 when the conductor said, "I'm afraid there's only room for four, sir. If you all want to stay together, you'll have to take Car 16. It's bigger, but you'd still better hurry."

Just then, Emily caught sight of Alice and her brother, Tom, waiting in line for the larger car. Alice saw her too.

"Emily, come with us!" she called.

"Can I, Father?" Emily asked. "Please?"

Father thought for a moment. "Very well," he said. "Hing can go with you. Here's the fare. We'll wait for you on the other side."

"Thank you!" Emily kissed him and her mother, said goodbye to her sisters, and ran off with Hing to join Alice.

Car 16 was every bit as crowded as Car 6. Once on board, the girls scrambled to the front while Tom climbed onto the roof. Hing decided to stay outside on the streetcar's rear platform.

More and more people clambered on board. Soon the platform was so packed that Emily lost sight of Hing. She was looking back, straining to find him, when she spotted Florence pushing her way through the crowd.

Emily's happy mood vanished. She whirled around and slouched down in her seat, praying that Florence would stay at the back of the car and not see them. Wasn't it enough that Florence had ruined her race? Did she have to ruin this part of the holiday too?

"Alice!" Florence's voice rose above the clamour and caught Alice's attention. Before Emily could stop her, Alice was waving and shouting, "Florence! Come up here!"

"There's no room," Emily muttered.

"There is if you move closer to the window," Alice said. "And it's important, because I talked to Florence yesterday about the race and she admitted the whole thing. She promised to tell you herself, and if she doesn't . . ."

Behind her, Emily could hear Florence saying, "Alice! I'm so glad—" Then her tone changed abruptly. "Oh . . . I didn't see Emily. I'm sorry. I'll go back and sit with my father."

"Stay here!" Alice pulled Florence onto the seat. "Remember what you promised. Go on, tell her! Or else I'll never speak to you again."

Florence leaned across Alice and, in a halting voice, said, "Emily . . . I'm sorry. About the race and . . . everything."

At that moment, the streetcar started up. The bell clanged and people's voices rose in anticipation.

Emily stared out the window and pretended she hadn't heard Florence. Soon they'd be in Esquimalt and she'd be with her family. Until then, she wanted to forget about the race and enjoy the streetcar ride with Alice. Maybe tomorrow she and Florence could make a fresh start at being friends.

As they were nearing the Point Ellice Bridge, the car slowed down to let Car 6 cross over first. It was stifling inside, with the afternoon sun beating through the windows and so many bodies pressed together. Emily asked the conductor to open her window, then leaned out as far as she could to breathe in the fresh air.

Up ahead, the bridge was busy with traffic. She counted three horse-drawn carriages and several people on foot. And there was George, coming up the street on his bicycle. "Alice, look!" she said. "George is going to bike across. He never told me he had a bicycle."

Alice leaned out beside her and the two waved excitedly. "Hello, George! We'll get there before you do!"

A man in the seat behind pulled out his pocket watch and grumbled, "It's ten minutes to two. Can't this car go any faster?"

"I can see Car 6," Emily said. "It's just reached the other side."

"About time," said the grumbler.

Slowly, Car 16 rolled onto the bridge. "We'll be lucky to get over with this load," the conductor remarked.

Emily took no notice of his words. What an adventure, taking the streetcar over the Gorge. And how brave of George to go on his bicycle. She was about to say as much to Alice when she heard a loud crack, like a gunshot. Her stomach lurched. Suddenly afraid, she reached for Alice's hand.

Then a second explosive crack split the air. Emily felt herself falling. The world turned into a terrifying confusion of arms and legs and bodies as the streetcar dropped through space and crashed into the water below.

Everything was dark.

Emily scarcely knew which way was up or down, but the car was underwater and water was pouring in and she knew she had to get out. Something was holding her—she wrenched herself free and, flailing her arms, discovered the open window above her head. She kicked her way out, then swam up through the water,

desperate to reach the surface. Almost there—
she had a sense of light—but then her head
bumped against something and she was forced
back down.

She tried again. The water was muddy, murky,
filled with debris, but this time she reached the
surface. With lungs bursting, she gasped for air
and gulped it in. A fragment of the shattered car
floated by. She lunged for it and held on. All
around her, people were groaning and screaming,
or floating silently, jammed between pieces of
broken ironwork or timber.

A leg rose up beside her—a girl's leg, with a
white stocking and a black button shoe.
Struggling to keep a grip on the floating wreckage,
Emily used her free hand to turn the girl upright,
then gasped in horror. Florence! But was she
dead or alive?

She couldn't look, she couldn't think. Frantically
she pulled Florence onto the wreckage. She tried
to hold on but no longer had the strength. All she
could do was close her eyes and let go.

CHAPTER N.º 10

Emily's thoughts drifted like ghosts, appeared and disappeared in a hazy world of water and light. She was lying in a boat, but who was rowing? Was it George? No . . . George was riding across the bridge. The bridge fell. George fell. Everyone fell.

She thought she could hear muffled cries and moans. She wanted to cry out—for her mother and father and sisters, for Hing, for Alice . . . She moved her lips and tasted salt. She tried to speak, but all she could manage was a moan.

Her teeth chattered. She couldn't stop shivering. She couldn't think why the sun felt so cold. Was she a ghost?

Water splashed beneath the oars. The rhythm lulled her into a drifting sleep.

The next thing she knew, Emily was lying on the ground, wrapped in a velvet curtain. People were moving about—hundreds, it seemed— and their voices were rising and falling around her.

"My daughters!" someone wailed. "Tell me, what's happened to my daughters?"

Someone else cried, "No, it can't be! My brother was right beside me!"

Then, "Alice! She can't be dead!"

Emily sat up abruptly. The blood rushed to her face and her pulse thudded in her ears. She remembered—the car, the bridge, the crash.

She remembered how she, Alice, and Florence had clasped each other, terrified, as the car went falling through space. Then it had tipped. Water had rushed in and she'd gone through the window, narrowly escaping the crush of people trying to get out the same way. She had left Alice behind. And Florence—but she'd seen her again. The button shoe, the wreckage . . .

She shuddered, stunned by what had happened. People were everywhere, lying or sitting on the ground, wandering about with dazed expressions, moving anxiously from person to person. She saw a row of bodies at the water's edge, young and old, men, women, and children. She turned away quickly, only to see the undertaker's wagon draw up at the gate.

A young woman came and knelt beside her. "What's your name, dear?"

Emily told her, then asked, "Who are you? Where am I?"

"I'm Miss Drake," the woman said kindly. "You're at Captain Grant's house and it's been turned into a hospital. They came that quick, the doctors. Other people, too, from all around, bringing clothes and blankets to help out. And when we ran out of blankets, Mrs. Grant took down her curtains, velvet and all." She wrapped the curtain more snugly around Emily and took her by the hand. "Come with me. We'll have a doctor look at you and find you some dry clothes."

"I want my mother." Emily started to cry. "Where's my mother?"

"Was she with you in the car?"

"No . . . only Alice and Florence. And Hing." Her body shook with tears.

"There, there." Miss Drake hugged her. "You've had a terrible shock, but now you're safe. You were lucky that boy came along when he did. I saw you slip under, but before I could reach you, he pulled you into his boat and brought you to shore."

As she was talking, Miss Drake was leading Emily towards the house. They'd almost reached the door when Emily looked over her shoulder and cried, "Hing!"

She ran across the lawn and into his outstretched arms. "You're alive?" she sobbed. "You're not a ghost?"

"No ghost," he said. "I fall, land in water. See? Clothes all wet! Hold on timber. Boat pick me up. Now you go in house. See doctor. Then we go home."

A short time later, Emily was in dry clothes and ready to leave. "I've got a bump on my head and some bruises," she told Hing. "The doctor said I was lucky."

"Very lucky," Hing said. "Many people not so lucky."

One of Captain Grant's neighbours offered them a ride home in his buggy. As they were driving by the approach to the collapsed bridge, they saw a huge gathering of people—some eager to be helpful, some frantic with anxiety, others in a state of shock. Emily and Hing scanned the crowd, hoping to catch a glimpse of her parents.

"Where are they?" Emily asked anxiously. "How will they know we're all right?"

"They'll have to cross back over on the railway bridge," their driver explained, "seeing as how they made it to the other side. I'll go back that way later and see if I can find them, let them know you're safe and sound."

As soon as they got home, Hing ordered Emily to drink some hot beef broth and promptly put her to bed.

"I'm not sleepy," she said. "I want to see Mother and Father."

"Sleep!" he said. "Family home soon. You wake up, you see."

"Hing . . . why did it happen?"

He didn't have an answer.

Emily tried to stay awake but couldn't. The last

thought she had before falling asleep was of the regatta, bright with colour and music and celebration. It already seemed like a lifetime ago.

It was noon the next day when Emily woke up. Jane and Amelia had clearly been watching and waiting, for the moment she opened her eyes they cried, "She's awake!" and hugged her.

Mother and Father rushed in and did the same.

At first, Emily was confused. "Am I late for school? What's—? Oh." She burst into tears. "Alice!" she cried. "I left Alice!"

"Alice is fine," Father said.

"She can't be! I heard someone say that she's dead!"

"No, dear. They must have meant another Alice. Your Alice is fine, except for a broken ankle. She got out the window after you but was hit by a piece of ironwork. A man picked her up and held her afloat until they were rescued. I saw her this morning. She's asking after you."

Emily sighed with relief. "And Florence?"

Her parents exchanged glances. "She's alive," Mother said. "And we've heard it's thanks to you. So Florence is fine . . . but her father was killed. Poor soul, he couldn't get out of the car."

On the Friday following the disaster, George and his parents came to call. And Emily learned that it was George who had saved her.

"But how?" she wondered. "I saw you on your bicycle."

"I'd just got onto the bridge when I heard the first crack," he explained. "Then I pedalled like mad to get off. I biked straight over to Captain Grant's place—it's right there at the bridge—and went out in his rowboat. He was already rescuing people with the men from his sealing schooner, using his company's boats.

"You know, there was a horse and buggy in front of me on the bridge, and that horse must have sensed something. Because even before I heard the crack, it wheeled around and ran back to the city side. Got there safely, but the buggy just ahead of it went down with a whole family. And Tom! You know he was on the roof of the car? Well, he was thrown off and landed in a clear patch of water. No wreckage in the way, nothing. He just swam to shore."

"We're hearing of so many miracles," George's father said. "Two people sitting side by side on the car, one drowns, the other escapes with no injuries whatsoever. And those poor people sitting on the left-hand side of the car, like Mr. Featherby-Jones . . ." He shook his head sadly. "They had no chance at all once the car tipped over."

"And heroes!" said George's mother. "The number of people who rushed to help, like our George, and Justice Drake's daughters, fine ladies working side by side with rough men from the shipyard. And many people who were thought to have drowned were resuscitated in the nick of time. Three Chinamen were rescued too, like your Hing. But oh, mercy, the lives lost, old and young alike . . ."

Emily looked up and caught her father gazing at her, his eyes bright with tears. She couldn't imagine what might have happened if her whole family had taken Car 16. And to think that they had seen the car go down, knowing that she was on board . . .

Father held out his hand. "Let's go and feed the ducks," he said. "Jane and Amelia, you can come too."

Normally, the girls would have skipped or run to the park, chatting and laughing all the way. Today they walked in silence.

A gloom had settled over the city. There wasn't a single person who wasn't affected in some way, who didn't know someone who had lost a loved one. Many houses had a black wreath on the door, a sign that the family within was mourning a lost parent or child. Flags that had fluttered so gaily on the morning of the disaster now drooped at half-mast. Except for a funeral procession of hearses and carriages on their way to the cemetery, the streets were empty.

They found the park deserted, but it wasn't long before they were surrounded by ducks and swans, eager for a handout. A mother duck paddled towards them, followed by a string of eight ducklings, desperate to keep up. Emily was surprised to catch herself laughing. Father laughed too, and his gold tooth gleamed in the sun.

In the days following the tragedy, everyone had a story to tell about a narrow escape. No one could explain why some people had been saved while others had not. But there was a clear explanation for the cause of the disaster.

"The city and its cost-cutting measures!" Father said one evening. "The Depression is no excuse. One inspector, with one month's experience, and how does he examine the bridge? First he rows under and then—"

"Father, please stop," Emily said. "I don't want to hear about it."

His face softened. "Of course you don't. I'm sorry. I do have some happier news. Hing has agreed to stay on until the end of June. He wants to make sure you're really all right. Otherwise, he says, he'll be worrying about you and not paying attention to his restaurant."

Emily smiled. The end of June was a whole month away.

CHAPTER N°12

Emily peeked through the kitchen doorway and watched Hing give the copper kettle one last shine. He had served his final meal at the Murdochs' home and done the washing up. Soon he would leave their house for the last time. But not before Emily gave him her surprise.

A few moments later, Father called Hing into the parlour. "We're sorry to see you go," he said. "But we wish you much prosperity, long life, and happiness." He handed Hing an envelope.

"And we have presents!" Amelia said excitedly.

"Show him, Emily!"

Emily reached for the red scroll lying on the table. With Jane's help, she unrolled it carefully, then held it up for Hing to see.

"It's for your restaurant," she said. "I hope you like the name. I did the calligraphy and Jane drew the dragon and the clouds."

"I coloured his scales," said Amelia.

"Ah, Em-ry." Hing's voice was filled with emotion. "Jane, Amelia—thank you. Mei Yuk Lung! Beautiful Jade Dragon! Perfect name for restaurant. Very lucky. Hing lucky, too. You good girls. Very special."

Try as she might, Emily couldn't hold back the tears.

"Don't cry!" Hing said. "You come visit in restaurant. Use chopsticks. You fast runner, you come on time. Promise?"

Emily promised and said, "You'll never have to beat the gong for me again."

CHAPTER N.º 13

Something was different. Something about Father.

Emily thought about this as she weeded the vegetable garden. She had first sensed it the day after Hing left. What with his leaving and school ending, she hadn't pursued the matter, but all week long it had bothered her. It was something small, but somehow important.

She had more chores to do now that Hing was gone, especially since he was not being replaced. But after helping Mother with the cooking and baking and so forth, she still had time to enjoy her summer holidays. She and Florence had been keeping Alice company since school ended, playing games and having tea parties. Alice's ankle was mending nicely, and soon she would be able to join them on walks to the park and to the beach.

With everything that had happened, it was impossible for Emily to hold a grudge against Florence. Besides, Florence wasn't really so bad, once you got to know her.

Emily also had George's birthday party to look forward to. But how would she feel, going back to the Gorge?

George had told her that he sometimes saw lights flickering across the water at the scene of the tragedy. And on nights when the waterway was empty, he thought he could hear the splashing of oars and the plaintive cries of children.

Emily shivered. If things had been different, if she and Alice had sat on the left side of the car instead of the right, if Hing hadn't stayed outside on the platform . . .

Just then, she noticed Florence riding up to her house. She left the weeding and walked over to greet her.

"I can't stay," Florence said, "but I wanted to give you this. The seat's too high for you but you can lower it."

"What?" Emily stared at the bicycle. "You don't mean—"

"Yes, you can have it," Florence said. "We're moving back to England next week, Mother and I. The house has been sold." She handed the bicycle to Emily. "It won't take you long to learn how to ride it. Just make sure you have someone holding on for a while."

"I don't know how to thank you," Emily said.

"Me either," said Florence, smiling, and she held out her arms for a hug.

Later that afternoon, Emily wheeled the bicycle down to the James Bay Bridge and waited for her father. The moment she saw him, she waved and called out, "Look, Father! Florence gave me her bicycle!"

His reaction took her by surprise. Instead of saying, "How splendid," or "Lucky girl," he threw his head back and laughed.

In that instant, Emily knew what was different. "Your tooth! Where's your gold tooth?"

"Oh, Emily!" He ruffled her hair. "You'll see soon enough."

When they got home he leaned her bicycle against the side of the shed, opened the door, and went inside. A moment later he came out with a royal-blue Rambler. "This is for you."

"Father! I thought . . . You always said we couldn't afford it."

"Yes, but the disaster at the bridge got me thinking. I knew how much you wanted a bicycle. And you are that precious, I decided you must have one, tough times or not. So I pulled together almost enough money, then sold my gold tooth to make up the difference."

"But your smile looks different, and I loved your gold tooth. And two bicycles! What will I do with two?"

"Keep one, give one away. You decide."

It was an easy decision. She pointed to the vermilion Raleigh and said, "I'll give that one to Alice and I'll keep the Rambler. But only if you teach me how to ride it."

His smile warmed her heart, even without the gold. "Hop on," he said. "I'll hold it steady and make sure you never fall."

NOTE

With fifty-five men, women, and children dead, and twenty-seven seriously injured, the streetcar disaster in Victoria on May 26, 1896, was an appalling tragedy. What made it even worse? It could have been prevented.

Car 16 was designed to carry sixty passengers, but on that day it carried over 140. The maximum weight that the bridge could bear was ten tons, but the estimated weight of the overloaded car was more than twice that amount.

Several survivors of the tragedy heard conductor Harry Talbot remark that they'd be lucky to get over the bridge with such a heavy load. He spoke from experience. Strangely enough, in 1893, he'd been the motorman in charge of Car 16 when, on the same holiday, the same bridge sagged four feet under the weight of the car.

After that near-disaster, boreholes were drilled to inspect the wooden beams. The holes were never filled. For three years, water collected inside and contributed to the rot that led to the ultimate collapse of the bridge.

The inspection that took place less than a month before the tragedy involved little more than a cursory look at the vibrations of passing traffic. Sadly, the inspector's five-year-old son was among the dead.

In the end, the City of Victoria and the streetcar company were found to be equally responsible. It was the worst streetcar accident ever to occur in North America.

BOOK THREE

Building Bridges

CHAPTER N.º 1

Emily feels the ground give way, feels herself falling down with the bridge and the streetcar, down, down into the Gorge. Water rushes in, pulling her deeper. As she struggles, Alice grabs hold of her arm and won't let go.

Then she sees Florence floating by, pulling a girl by the hand—not up to the surface but down to the bottom. Florence smiles and says, "Look who I'm taking with me."

Emily looks and sees her own face staring back at her. The eyes are glazed with horror. The mouth is fixed in a scream . . .

Emily woke up sharply, the sound of the scream still ringing in her ears.

Within seconds, her mother was at her side, drawing her close. "There, there, Emily," she murmured. "It's all right."

"No, it's not." Emily choked back a sob. "Florence didn't move back to England. She drowned and I drowned and Alice . . ."

"No, dear. It's only a dream." Mother tucked her in and kissed her. "Go back to sleep. You'll get over your nightmares in time. You'll see."

But when? she wondered. And how?

When Emily awoke again in the morning, the questions were still on her mind. So too was the memory of the disaster that triggered the night-mares—the collapse of the bridge that sent an overcrowded streetcar, on which she and her friends were passengers, plunging into the waters of the Gorge.

It was now New Year's Day, 1897. Nearly eight months had passed since the disaster at Point Ellice Bridge, but the fear Emily had felt that day was still with her. During the summer, her nightmares had been so frequent and her cries so alarming that they'd consistently woken up the household. In the fall they had seemed to ease off, much to everyone's relief. But with the coming of winter and the approach of the new year, they were back again.

Emily thought she knew why. And, as the day progressed, she grew more and more anxious.

"Do we *have* to go to the Walshes' for dinner?" she kept asking. "Why can't we stay here?"

Try as she might, she could not convince her parents to change their plans. And that afternoon she found herself on a streetcar bound for the scene of the disaster.

Emily hadn't been near the Gorge since that terrible day. She'd almost gone in August, to her friend George Walsh's birthday party, but a stomach ache had kept her at home. The thought of going there now made her shudder.

Her younger sister Jane noticed her discomfort and patted her hand. "Don't be scared," she said.

"And don't worry," little Amelia said seriously.

"Your sisters are right," said Father. "It's a brand-new year. Let's put all our worries and fears behind us. What do you say?" He squeezed her shoulder as the streetcar drew up to the new Point Ellice Bridge and stopped to let them off. "Chin up! We'll cross each bridge as we come to it."

Emily dutifully stuck out her chin. At least she didn't have to cross *this* bridge—not today, anyway.

As the streetcar clanged its bell and went on its way, rolling onto the bridge, she turned quickly, refusing to look at the churning waters of the Gorge.

On the short walk to the Walshes' they passed another reminder of the tragedy—the home where Emily had been taken after her rescue. She hastened her step as the unwelcome memories began to flood in. The lawn, the bodies, the cries of anguish . . .

"Don't think about it," Mother said, as if reading Emily's mind. She gave her a reassuring hug.

It wasn't long before they reached the Walshes' house, where a large crowd had gathered to welcome in the new year.

George grabbed Emily's hand and tugged her away to his room. "Wait till you see my Christmas presents," he said.

"We want to see, too!" Jane followed, with Amelia at her heels.

He showed them his croquet set, complete with candle sockets attached to the wickets so they could play at night, and a new archery set.

"Are these arrows really—ouch!" cried Amelia.

"Yes, they're sharp!" Emily scolded. "You're not supposed to touch."

George laughed. "We can shoot arrows the next time you come."

"I'd rather play croquet," said Emily.

"I've got a new board game, too," said George. "Do you want to play?"

Soon all four were happily involved in a game of Snakes and Ladders.

As the afternoon wore on, and the guests were called to sit down for a festive dinner, Emily couldn't help but think back to the previous year, when the celebration had been at her house. That was when she'd first met George. What a trouble-maker he'd been then. To think that only a few months later, he would save her life!

During dinner there was the usual boring talk among the grown-ups, with a lot of big words Emily didn't understand. Last year she'd over-heard Father talking about an economic slump and tough times ahead. His words had proved to be true. Now he was saying that 1897 could mark a turnaround for the province.

The other guests agreed, voicing their opinions about the new parliament buildings, the booming mining industry in the interior, the construction of new railway lines . . .

Emily stifled a yawn.

Across the table, George was trying to make her and her sisters laugh, first by waggling his eyebrows, then by wiggling his ears. Jane looked back at him, cross-eyed. Amelia stuck out her tongue. Emily had to put her napkin to her mouth to hold in the giggles.

The end of the meal brought on the usual toasts, beginning, as always, with one to Queen Victoria. "The Queen!" Mr. Walsh said. "In the year of her Diamond Jubilee. Sixty glorious years on the throne."

Everyone stood up, raised his glass, and repeated, "The Queen! On her Diamond Jubilee!"

There was a buzz of excitement as they discussed the celebrations being planned to mark the occasion, not only in Victoria but throughout the entire British Empire.

"The 24th of May won't be nearly so grand this year," someone said. "All the stops are being pulled out for the Jubilee in June."

"From what I've heard," a newcomer to Victoria remarked, "the 24th of May wasn't so grand last year. Wasn't it just out here, on the Gorge—?"

"Don't!" Emily burst out without thinking.

A heavy silence fell over the room.

"Oh, dear," the man said. "I am sorry."

Mr. Walsh cleared his throat. "Another toast is in order. To the memory of those who lost their lives in the disaster. To those who mourn their loss. And to those who survived."

"And to Emily," George said earnestly. He raised his glass in her direction and the others followed suit.

Emily blushed to the tips of her ears. It was the first time she'd ever been toasted.

That night, as the girls were lying in bed, Amelia asked, "What's a *diamond julibee*? Is it like a necklace?"

"It's *jubilee*," Emily corrected. "And it's not jewellery, it's a celebration. Queen Victoria's been the Queen for sixty years, and that's why it's called 'diamond.' When she was Queen for fifty years, it was the Golden Jubilee."

"What happened at the *golden julibee*?"

"Amelia, it's *jubilee!* And I don't remember. I was only a year old."

"Queen Victoria's been the Queen for a long time," said Jane. "Even before Mother and Father were born."

"Listen, Em," Amelia piped up. "I know another *julibee*."

"Jubilee!"

"It's your birthday—on January 28. You'll be eleven. You'll be too old to have nightmares."

Emily could only hope that she was right.

CHAPTER N° 2

"Make a wish!" said Alice.

Emily looked at the shining candles on her cake and thought for a moment. She already had her bicycle. All she wanted now was an end to the nightmares. She made her wish and blew out the candles in one breath.

Amelia clapped her hands. "Happy *julibee*, Emily!"

Emily smiled. She no longer bothered to correct her sister. In fact, she was beginning to think that *julibee* should be a proper word, used for all manner of festive occasions.

It certainly described her birthday. She'd ridden to school that morning in a colourful whirl of red, pink, yellow, and blue, thanks to the ribbons her sisters had secretly tied onto the spokes of her bicycle wheels. Alice, her very best friend, had come for supper and given her a new bell for her bicycle. Jane and Amelia had drawn her a picture to hang on their bedroom wall. It showed Emily biking along the waterfront, accompanied by leaping whales, a soaring eagle, and a flock of seagulls. Her parents had given her a box of watercolours and told her that, come April, she'd be taking art lessons along with Jane. This was a pleasant surprise for both girls! And Mother had made Emily's favourite dinner—roast beef with Yorkshire pudding and mashed potatoes, and birthday cake for dessert.

Emily was about to have a second helping of cake when she heard a knock at the back door.

"It's Hing!" she exclaimed. It was her first birthday without Hing, who had once been her family's cook, and she missed him. But Hing had finally been able to bring his family to Canada, and Emily was looking forward to meeting his daughter, Mei Yuk. Maybe Hing had brought Mei Yuk to surprise her!

"Manners, Emily!" Father called as she ran from the room. "It's not a race!"

Emily flung open the door and greeted Hing with a hug. He hadn't brought Mei Yuk, but at least he hadn't forgotten her birthday.

"Come in!" she said. "Do you want some of my birthday cake? It's a tipsy cake, with custard and almonds."

"No cake, please," Hing said. "No time. Restaurant very busy. But here. Happy birthday." He handed her a box of his tasty lemon tarts and a brightly decorated scroll. "For Chinese New Year. Next week, Year of Rooster. You and family come to Beautiful Jade Dragon Restaurant at noon for New Year banquet. I already speak to your father. It is all arranged."

"And then can I meet Mei Yuk?" Emily asked.

Hing smiled proudly. "You can meet whole Hing family!"

All week long Emily thought about Mei Yuk. What would she be like? She already knew that Hing's youngest child had been born in the Year of the Dog, the same year as she was. According to Hing, that meant that both girls could be selfish and stubborn. But they were also honest, loyal, and industrious—and champions of justice.

Emily pictured the two of them visiting the shops in Chinatown, sampling the New Year's treats and collecting the "lucky money" in *lai see* envelopes. Maybe they could even go to a Chinese opera together!

On the morning of the Chinese New Year, Emily ate a hurried breakfast, finished her chores, and set off on her bicycle. The rest of her family would be at Hing's restaurant at noon, but Emily just couldn't wait.

Chinatown was bursting with firecrackers when she arrived, and throngs of people were gathering to usher in the Year of the Rooster. At Hing's busy restaurant, every table was occupied. Emily looked around and saw two young waiters bustling among the customers, loaded down with platters of food. They paused when they saw her, exchanged a few words in Cantonese, and grinned broadly.

"You . . . Em-ry!" the younger one said. "Yes?"

"Yes," she replied. Then it dawned on her. "You must be Hing's sons."

"Hing, yes! Now . . . wait, please." The older one served his customers and disappeared behind a bamboo curtain. A short time later he returned with Hing.

"Em-ry, meet my sons!" Hing beamed. "Bak Cheun, number-one son. Gum Gin, number-two son. I told them to watch for a little girl with yellow hair, pink cheeks, and bicycle."

"Welcome to Victoria, British Columbia, Canada," Emily said. "I'm pleased to meet you. But where is Mei Yuk?"

At the mention of Mei Yuk, Hing and the boys looked at one another with grave expressions. "Sorry, Em-ry," Hing said. "Mei Yuk upstairs. Very shy. Afraid to come down."

"I could go upstairs and see her," Emily offered. "May I?"

Hing's face brightened. "This way," he said. "Stairs through kitchen."

Emily followed him into the kitchen, where a woman stood over the stove, frying bite-sized portions of meat and vegetables.

"My wife," Hing said proudly.

She looked up from her cooking and gave Emily a warm smile. *"Gung hey fat choy!"*

"Welcome to Victoria," Emily said. *"Gung hey fat choy!"*

Hing showed her the stairs, and she soon found herself in a small room above the kitchen. Adjoining it was another room with two windows and a door that opened onto a balcony. Both rooms were crammed with rough bits of furniture. A door laid out on two sawhorses formed a table, and an assortment of crates served as chairs. Elsewhere, Emily noticed a stack of faded quilts and a few pictures that she thought might be of Chinese gods. There was no sign of a person.

"Hello!" She waited, but there was no answer. She was about to leave when a faint rustling caught her attention. "Mei Yuk?"

A small girl dressed in red crept out from behind a carved wooden screen. She glanced at Emily from beneath her bangs, then lowered her head and stared fixedly at the floor.

It wasn't the reception Emily had been expecting.

"Gung hey fat choy," she said. "I'm Emily." Mei Yuk did not look up, but Emily pressed on. "I like your dress. It's red for good luck, isn't it? For Chinese New Year."

There was still no response. But why would

there be? Emily chided herself. Mei Yuk didn't understand English.

She tried another approach. "Do you want to collect some *lai see* envelopes with me, and see the firecrackers?" She extended her hand, hoping that Mei Yuk would at least understand the gesture. But instead of accepting Emily's hand, Mei Yuk shook her head firmly and scurried back to her hiding place.

Crushed with disappointment and confused by Mei Yuk's reaction, Emily went back downstairs. What did I do wrong? she wondered. She'd sent Mei Yuk letters and lucky money and wanted to be her friend. So why didn't Mei Yuk like her?

As she entered the kitchen, Hing and his wife looked up hopefully. Their expressions faded, however, when they saw that she was alone.

"No Mei Yuk?" said Hing's wife.

"No," Emily said sadly.

Hing sighed. "Maybe after New Year, when everything is quiet. Come back then, see Mei Yuk."

Only if she wants to see me, Emily said to herself.

"But today, at noon, you come with family," Hing went on. "Special banquet for New Year." He gestured to the pieces of chicken spread out on the chopping block. "Chicken bring many good things in the new year. And make you run fast! Ready for next race."

Emily smiled, remembering the dishes that he'd cooked to prepare her for the Victoria schools' sports day: rice for energy, chicken for strength and speed. She hoped he could cook something special for Mei Yuk, something that might give her courage.

Since Mei Yuk wouldn't join her, Emily visited a few shops by herself, sampling the nuts and sweets offered by the merchants and collecting her own *lai see* envelopes. Then she stood outside Hing's and watched the long strings of firecrackers exploding in ear-splitting bursts and covering the ground with bits of red paper.

When Emily's family arrived at the restaurant,

Hing welcomed them and showed them to a special table.

"Did you meet Mei Yuk?" Mother asked, after they were seated.

Emily nodded. "But she hardly even looked at me. She made me feel like a bully."

"She hasn't been here very long," Father reminded her. "It's a big adjustment for her, for all of them, being in a new country. Especially when they can't speak the language."

"And don't forget," Mother added, "she scarcely knows her own father. He's like a stranger. When you think about it, Hing knows you better than he knows Mei Yuk."

"Maybe she's jealous," Jane remarked.

"She needn't be," said Emily. "I only want to be friends."

"Don't push too hard," Father said. "Give her time."

"Bother time," Emily muttered. Why did everything important have to take time?

CHAPTER N° 3

A few days later, Emily and Alice were sprawled across Emily's bed, reading her mother's latest magazine from England. It had a special section for girls, with contests and activities as well as advice, some of which Emily tried to follow.

"Listen to this, Alice," she said. "'Are you helping someone else to have a good time? The root of perfect pleasure is unselfishness.'"

"I thought it was having a bicycle," Alice teased.

Emily ignored her and read on. "'The cheery, bright, everyday girl with no accomplishments to boast of—except for the great attraction of thoughtfulness for others—is the one who can provide the oil that makes the wheel of life go round smoothly.' Goodness, what a confusing sentence."

"What does it mean?" Alice asked.

"It means you should be nice to people," Emily said. "Especially if you don't have any accomplishments."

"You've got accomplishments," Alice pointed out. "Is that why you weren't nice to Florence?"

"I *was* nice to Florence," Emily argued. "I saved her life, didn't I?"

"I meant before that."

"Alice, *she* wasn't nice to *me*. Not at first. She was always leaving me out of things. And then she made me trip so she could beat me in the school race." She paused. "I dream about her, you know. We're in the streetcar, you and me and Florence, and the water—"

"What's a wheel of life?" Alice abruptly changed the subject.

Emily sighed. She longed to talk to Alice about the disaster. After all, Alice had been on the streetcar with her, and she'd nearly drowned too. She was the only person Emily knew who could really understand what she'd been through. But Alice refused to discuss it. For her, it was as if the events of that day had never happened.

"A wheel of life?" Emily repeated. "I'm not sure, but it's given me an idea. Remember what I told you about Mei Yuk, and how scared she was when she saw me? Well, I'm going to be the oil that makes her life run smoothly."

Alice frowned. "What do you mean, you're going to be the oil?"

"Not *real* oil. It's like—what was that word we learned in composition? When you compare one thing with something else. Not a semaphore . . ."

"A metaphor!" Alice said. "Now I see. Can I help with Mei Yuk? Maybe we could have a party."

"Yes!" said Emily. "A Welcome to Victoria party!"

They warmed to the idea, but decided to wait a few weeks in order to give Mei Yuk more time to learn English.

"I'll go to Chinatown with you and help teach her," Alice said. "If Ma lets me."

"Let's go on Saturday," Emily suggested. "We'll teach her all the words she'll need to know for our party. Like *pin the tail on the donkey* and *blind-man's buff*."

"And *charades* and *raspberry cordial*."

"And we'll call our party . . ." Emily thought for a moment, then remembered what Mei Yuk's name meant in English. "We'll call it the Beautiful Jade Jubilee!"

"I'm not allowed to go," Alice grumbled the following day. Emily had stopped to get Alice on her way to school, and they were walking their bicycles together. "Ma says that Chinatown is a filthy den of iniquity, whatever that means. And it's full of unsavoury heathens who do nothing but gamble and smoke opium. And she's never even been there! It's a good thing she never found out about the time we went with George and Tom."

Emily agreed. Then she said, "Would it help if my mother spoke to your mother?"

Alice shook her head. "It's not only her. It's Pa, too. And once they make up their minds . . . Are you still going?"

"Of course," said Emily. "My mother doesn't mind, as long as I go straight to Hing's and come straight home. Hing thinks it might help Mei Yuk. Father told him to expect me on Saturday morning." She grinned. "It'll be like playing school, only I'll have a real pupil."

The pupil in question looked none too eager when Emily arrived on Saturday morning. She was in the kitchen washing dishes and did not even glance in Emily's direction. Nor did she stop working.

A stern word from her mother made her look up from her task. And, after Hing launched into a stream of Cantonese, she nodded reluctantly, dried her hands, and trudged upstairs.

"I tell her, speak English for two hours," Hing explained.

"Good," Emily said. "I can teach her a lot in two hours."

Upstairs, she was encouraged to find Mei Yuk sitting at the makeshift table instead of hiding behind the screen.

"I am sitting down," Emily said, joining her. "Can you say that?"

Mei Yuk gave her a blank look.

"I am sitting down." Emily repeated the words in a louder voice, but got another blank look— this time, with a hint of fear.

She lowered her voice and tried again. "You are sitting down."

Mei Yuk stared at her hands.

"I am standing up." Emily did so, but Mei Yuk didn't raise her eyes.

Exasperated, Emily pointed to herself, and then to Mei Yuk. "Me. You. Mei Yuk. Beautiful Jade. Can you say it in English? Me, Emily. You, Mei Yuk. Father, Hing. Can you say that? Hing. Father."

A tear rolled down Mei Yuk's cheek.

"Oh, no!" Emily wailed. "Please don't cry! I didn't mean to upset you." Taking out her hand-kerchief, she leaned across the table and wiped away the tear. "There," she said softly. She took consolation in one small victory—at least Mei Yuk hadn't flinched or run away.

What to do next? She'd made her pupil cry and hadn't taught her a single thing. She was hopeless as a teacher, and hopeless at making Mei Yuk's life run smoothly. But the two hours weren't over yet. There was time to try something else.

"I am sitting down," she said. "Now I am standing up. Sit down, stand up. A toast to Mei Yuk!" She raised an imaginary glass and saw Mei Yuk's eyes flicker. "You're watching now, aren't you? Well then, goodbye!" She walked behind the wooden screen, waited for a moment and returned to the table. "Hello, Mei Yuk. I'm Emily. I am sitting down." Then, "I am standing up. Goodbye!" She went through the motions again and again. Sit down, stand up. Hello, goodbye.

She was nothing if not stubborn—a true sign of someone born in the Year of the Dog. The trouble was, Mei Yuk had the same trait.

On what felt like the hundredth time, she caught Mei Yuk holding her hand to her mouth. Her eyes were shining.

"Are you laughing at me?" Emily said. "Well, good." She bowed with a theatrical flourish. "Thank you, thank you."

"Thank . . . you," Mei Yuk whispered.

"What's that?" Emily cupped a hand to her ear. "Did you say something? Did you say thank you?"

Mei Yuk covered her mouth again, but not before Emily saw her smile.

"You're welcome!" she said. "Thank you. You're welcome."

Now what? Suddenly, charades came to mind. She played the part of a clown, clutching her belly and shaking with laughter. "Laugh! Ho, ho! Can you say that, Mei Yuk? Laugh!" Next, she acted out "cry," with a sorrowful face and exaggerated sobs. "Boo, hoo! Cry!"

"Cly," Mei Yuk said shyly.

"Yes!" Emily whooped with delight. "Laugh, cry, hello, goodbye!"

Before long, Mei Yuk was chanting along with her, still timidly, but no longer covering her mouth or staring at the floor. And Emily didn't mind that Mei Yuk's pronunciation wasn't perfect, or that she mixed up the *l* and *r* sounds. *Her-ro* for *hello* was good enough for Emily.

When Hing appeared, Mei Yuk surprised him and Emily by saying, "Hello, Father. Thank you."

Hing's smile widened. "Em-ry good teacher!"

Emily warmed at his praise but felt somewhat guilty. In all that time she'd hardly taught Mei Yuk anything. She was facing a monumental task. How would she manage next week?

Well, as Father would say, she'd cross that bridge when she came to it. If only Alice were there to help. They could act out all sorts of words and situations. Mei Yuk seemed to enjoy the charades part. But Emily couldn't teach *everything* that way. She'd be worn out.

Emily said goodbye to Mei Yuk—for real this time—and made her way out through the kitchen. As she left the restaurant she was hit by a strong, boiled-potato smell, a sure sign that opium was being cooked in at least one of the many opium factories. She'd once asked her father why people smoked opium, and he'd told her that it gave them dreams. Emily couldn't understand it. She'd give anything *not* to have dreams.

She wondered about Mei Yuk's dreams. Did she dream about China? Did she have nightmares about being in a new country? Did she miss her friends? There was so much Emily wanted to know.

It suddenly occurred to her that she'd hardly ever seen children in Chinatown. No wonder Mei Yuk seemed sad. She had no one to play with.

Right then and there, Emily came up with a new plan. An even better plan, because next time Alice would be able to help. And, best of all, it would give Mei Yuk a chance to have some fun.

CHAPTER N°. 4

The following Saturday, Mei Yuk came to Emily's house. Everything had been arranged. Her brother Bak Cheun brought her and promised to fetch her in two hours' time.

After Emily had introduced Mei Yuk to her family, the girls set off for Alice's house. Emily chatted and pointed out various things along the way, hoping that Mei Yuk might remember at least a few new words.

"That's a house," she said. "And a tree . . ." *House, tree, streetcar, buggy, horse, bird* . . . so many words! "See the sun, Mei Yuk? It's sunny."

"Sun," Mei Yuk echoed. "Sunny."

"Good!" Emily smiled. "It's mild today, too. It's almost the end of February and it feels like spring. Look, there's an eagle! And seagulls!" She drew Mei Yuk's attention to a bald eagle being mobbed by a swarm of seagulls.

Mei Yuk gave her a worried look.

"It's all right," Emily said. "They can't hurt the eagle. He's too big. But they pester him something fierce, the bullies."

A moment later, the eagle landed at the top of a fir tree and added its screeching cry to that of the gulls. Mei Yuk pointed excitedly. "Eagle? Tree?"

"Yes, Mei Yuk! You're learning fast. Now, see that house with the blue trim? That's Alice's house."

They had no sooner stepped into the yard than Tom and George appeared. Tom took one look at Mei Yuk and sneered. "Who's that?"

"Mei Yuk," said Emily. "Hing's daughter."

"What are you doing with her?"

"I'm playing with her and teaching her English."

"So what's she doing here? You can't take her inside our house."

"I wouldn't want to!" Emily flared up angrily. "Anyway, I'm only coming to get Alice. We're going to the park."

"Not with Alice. Ma won't let her go with a—"

"Be quiet!" Emily snapped. The thought that Tom might spoil things, just when Mei Yuk was beginning to open up, was enough to get her blood boiling.

"Come on, Tom," George said. He gave Emily an apologetic shrug and pulled Tom away. "Let's bike over to my place."

"You're wasting your time," Tom flung over his shoulder. "Alice won't go near one of those heathens."

"You don't even know what a heathen is!" Emily was determined to have the last word.

At that moment, Alice called out from an upstairs window, "Go on without me, Em. I'll meet you at the hill."

Her words made Emily wonder if Tom had been right. But she walked on with Mei Yuk and tried not to worry.

They had just reached the hill when Alice came running up. "Sorry," she said. "I had to help Ma with the dusting."

Emily smiled with relief. "So you were allowed to come?"

"Of course! Why not?"

"Well, Tom said . . ."

"Oh, bosh! Don't listen to what he says." She turned her attention to Mei Yuk. "Hello, Mei Yuk. I'm Alice Kerr."

Mei Yuk smiled shyly. "Hello," she said.

"Let's go up the hill," said Emily. "See, Mei Yuk?" She pointed to the summit. "Hill. Beacon Hill."

"Beacon Hill!" Mei Yuk grinned.

Suddenly they heard a high-spirited voice cry out, "Make way below!"

The girls looked up and gaped. "It's a lady!" Emily shrieked. "She's rolling down the hill!"

Rolling down Beacon Hill was a favourite pastime, but it was something that children did, not grown-up ladies. This lady might have been as old as *thirty!* They could even see her petticoat!

A black retriever bounded after her, barking excitedly.

By now the lady had stopped rolling and was getting to her feet, brushing bits of dirt and grass off her long, dark skirt. She saw the girls staring but didn't seem the least bit embarrassed. "What fun!" she said. "I've been wanting to do that for ages."

The dog woofed as if in agreement and cast a hopeful look to the top of the hill.

"Not now, Watch," the lady said, giving him a pat. "We'll come back another day." She smoothed her skirt and tucked a few loose strands of dark, curly hair into place. "Best thing for your health," she said, her eyes sparkling. "A good roll down a hill."

Still amazed, the girls watched her stride away. "Who is she?" Alice wondered.

"I don't know," said Emily. "But imagine, being grown-up and rolling down a hill."

"Wait till I tell Ma." Alice giggled. "She'll say it's scandalous."

"And it is!" Emily yelped. "Let's do it, too!"

And they all three went rolling down Beacon Hill.

After feeding the ducks, the girls strolled back to Alice's house, where she invited them in for a cup of cocoa. They were sitting at the kitchen table enjoying themselves when Mrs. Kerr walked in.

"A word, Alice, if you please," she said curtly.

Alice excused herself and followed her mother into the hall.

Emily couldn't help but overhear their conversation. She grew hot with a mixture of anger and shame. Thank goodness Mei Yuk couldn't understand.

"I won't have her in the house," Mrs. Kerr was saying. "Whatever were you thinking? She'll have to leave."

"But she's Emily's friend," Alice protested. "And my friend, too. We're teaching her English."

"Might as well teach a goose," her mother snorted. "I won't have it, Alice. If your father finds out . . . And as for the cup she's using, you be sure to wash it twice, in scalding water. She's probably contagious. Chinatown is a filthy, disease-ridden—"

"But Emily—"

"That's another thing. As long as Emily . . ." She lowered her voice.

Emily couldn't bear to hear any more. Seeing that Mei Yuk had finished her cocoa, she took the two cups and placed them side by side on the counter. Let Mrs. Kerr figure out which was which.

"Goodbye, Alice," she called out. "Thank you for the cocoa."

"Thank you," Mei Yuk said in her turn. "Goodbye."

Some goose! Emily smiled with pride.

It took more than Mrs. Kerr's words to discourage Emily from her goal. Every Saturday morning Bak Cheun would bring Mei Yuk to Emily's house to learn English. If it wasn't raining, the girls went to the park or to the beach. Otherwise, they stayed indoors. Alice sometimes met them on their outings or joined them at Emily's, but there were no more invitations to her house.

When Emily told Alice that she'd overheard her mother's remarks, Alice flushed with embarrassment and said she was sorry.

"As long as you don't feel the same way," Emily said. "You don't, do you?"

After a slight hesitation, Alice said, "No . . ."

It wasn't quite the wholehearted assurance Emily had been expecting.

CHAPTER Nº 5

For a while, Emily hoped that the time she was spending with Mei Yuk would put the Point Ellice Bridge disaster out of her mind and bring an end to her nightmares. But they continued.

One Saturday, after Emily had had a particularly bad night, Mei Yuk asked if she was feeling all right.

"I'm tired," Emily admitted. "I keep having nightmares."

"What is *nightmare*?" Mei Yuk asked.

"I'll show you." Emily pretended to fall asleep, waited a moment and woke up with a loud scream. "That's a nightmare," she said. "A very bad dream."

Mei Yuk nodded gravely. "Me, too. Nightmare. Very many people. Father, Mother, brother, nowhere. I cry many tear. I . . . found?"

"I think you mean lost," Emily said. She gave Mei Yuk's hand a sympathetic squeeze.

The next day, when Emily got home from Sunday School, Hing and Mei Yuk were waiting. They handed her two identical pictures showing a Chinese warrior from ancient times. He had a ferocious scowl, a dagger at his waist, and several gruesome objects hanging from his belt, including a skull.

"For nightmare," Mei Yuk explained.

Emily was puzzled. It was the sort of picture that might cause *more* nightmares.

"There's a story," Hing said. He told her about a Chinese emperor who had once had a terrible time with nightmares. Night after night he'd woken up screaming. Finally he'd ordered two of his fiercest warriors to stand guard outside his bedroom door and scare away the nightmares. His plan worked, and he was able to sleep.

But the warriors grew weary. All night long they stood on guard. All day long they fought in battles. They finally decided to hang pictures of themselves outside the Emperor's door instead, so that they could get some sleep.

"Now called Door Guardians," Hing said, pointing to the pictures. "As good as real warriors. Scare away your nightmares."

That night, Emily tacked the pictures on either side of her bedroom door, hoping she'd have a peaceful sleep. But again she woke up in the dark, her heart racing, another vision of deep water and a feeling of helplessness fading slowly from her mind.

The Door Guardians might have worked for that emperor, she thought, but they are certainly not helping me.

On the first Saturday in April, Alice showed up at Emily's. Two weeks had gone by since she'd last seen Mei Yuk, and she was surprised by her progress.

"Father talk English," Mei Yuk said. "Em-ry good teacher. Monday, school."

"I know," Alice groaned. "I hate Mondays."

"It's not that, Alice," Emily said excitedly. "She means that she's going to school on Monday."

"What? Where?"

"South Park! She's going to be in our class. It's all arranged."

"Why *our* school?"

"Because she knows me and I can help her, and it's not that far for her to come. Maybe in a couple of weeks we can finally have our party. Remember, the Beautiful Jade Jubilee?" Something in Alice's expression made her pause. "You still want to, don't you?"

"Yes, but . . ."

"Charade!" Mei Yuk broke in. "Can we play?"

Emily readily agreed, relieved that Mei Yuk had changed the subject.

They played until it was time for Alice to go home for dinner. She and Emily were on the porch, saying goodbye, when they saw Tom walking down the street. Alice quickly stepped back inside the house.

"What's the matter?" Emily asked.

"Nothing . . ."

Emily had an inkling. "You're not allowed to come over, are you? As long as I'm seeing Mei Yuk. Your mother—"

"It's not just Ma." Alice looked away, clearly uncomfortable. "Pa belongs to some group that doesn't like the Chinese."

"Well . . . what if he finds out you're coming here anyway?"

"I'll probably get a licking."

"What?" Emily was shocked. She knew that Alice's father had a temper, but to punish Alice for something like *that*? "Then you can't come." She spoke without hesitation. She wouldn't be

responsible for her best friend getting in trouble at home. "You'll just have to wait until Mei Yuk's not here."

"I could come back after dinner," Alice said. "Mei Yuk goes home at noon, doesn't she?"

"Yes, but my art lessons start this afternoon. Jane and I are going together. Didn't I tell you?"

"No." Alice looked hurt. "You don't tell me anything any more."

"Oh, Alice. Don't feel badly. Mei Yuk's lessons won't go on forever. She's such a fast learner, and once she starts school she won't need extra lessons from me. Pretty soon we can spend every Saturday morning together, just like before."

"Promise?"

"Of course. You're my best friend, remember? Nothing can change that."

CHAPTER N.º 6

"I hope Miss Carr won't think I'm too hopeless," Emily said as she and Jane set off for their art class. She was excited, but a little apprehensive. After all, their teacher wasn't just a teacher. She was a real artist. She'd studied art in San Francisco. She'd even won first prize for a drawing at the Victoria Fall Fair.

Miss Carr lived close to Beacon Hill Park, so it wasn't long before they were knocking on her door.

A stern-looking woman appeared. "If you're here for my sister's art lessons," she said, "they're in the old cow barn."

"The barn?" The girls raised their eyebrows.

"Out the back," she said, and closed the door.

"Does 'old cow barn' mean an old cow or an old barn?" Jane wondered as they walked around to the back.

"I don't know," said Emily. "But there's an old barn. And listen."

The sound of children's voices and laughter drifted down from high up in the barn.

"That's George!" Emily said, recognizing his familiar laugh. "I hope he behaves."

"The lessons must be in the hayloft," Jane remarked. "We'll have to go up the stairs."

A newly built wooden staircase led up the outer wall of the barn to a wide double door in the loft. The girls had almost reached the top of the stairs when a dog burst out onto the landing, followed by a pleasant-looking woman.

"Hello, girls," she said. "You must be Jane and Emily."

Emily took one look at the round, rosy face

and dark, curly hair and blurted out, "You're the lady I saw rolling down the hill!" Goodness! And she was their teacher?

"Quite right," the woman laughed. "I'm Miss Carr. A dedicated roly-poly. And I'm an Emily too, like you."

Emily beamed.

"Come in and join the others, Jane and Emily Too. Sit wherever you like. It's not raining so there's no need to worry about the skylight leaking. And don't mind the dog. Watch loves company."

Watch gave a friendly woof and wagged his tail.

There were six pupils, including George, and everyone was given a sketch pad, a pencil, and a stick of charcoal.

"Use your pencils and draw what you see," Miss Carr said, indicating the various objects she'd placed on the table. An apple. A plaster hand. A plaster foot. A stuffed raven. Emily drew the objects as faithfully as she could, but took time to observe her surroundings.

The converted loft, high in the middle and low at the sides, was rustic with its knotholed floor and burlap-covered walls. A big coal-oil lamp hung from a rafter, so Miss Carr could work at night, Emily supposed. Her teacher's paints and brushes, sketches and canvases were spread across a smaller table or stacked against the walls.

It was cozy in the studio, bright and warm with a fire crackling in the woodstove. The smells of hay and apples and new-sawn wood rose from below, and Emily could hear a cow chewing and the clucking of chickens. There was also the chatter and laughter of Miss Carr and her pupils. It wasn't a bit like school. Miss Carr even surprised them once and a while by singing out loud!

Every so often the shrill cry of a peacock filled the room, followed by a series of angry yaps from Watch. The first time this happened, Miss Carr explained that the peacock had come from Beacon Hill Park and was making his daytime quarters on the studio roof. "He likes to strut before the dormer window," she said. "He uses it as a mirror! And he loves to get a rise out of Watch. Silly old dog. You'd think he'd know by now."

After finishing his sketch of the raven, George asked, "Can we draw Watch?"

"I'd have to stuff him first," Miss Carr replied. She laughed as her pupils gasped with horror. "You sillies! You know I'd never do such a thing. And of course you may draw him. Watch loves to pose."

At the end of the first hour, Miss Carr left the studio and returned a few minutes later with a basket of fresh bread. "One slice is all you need for now," she said.

Only one slice? Emily swallowed her disappointment. At least they were thick slices. Would there be butter, too? Devonshire cream? Strawberry preserves? She grinned at Jane across the table. Mother hadn't mentioned that their art lessons would include snacks.

"Now tear it into chunks," said Miss Carr.

Emily frowned but followed the instructions. Then she sampled a piece. It tasted as good as it smelled.

"We're going to draw with charcoal," Miss Carr explained. "Charcoal will free things up, give you the lights and the darks. Study the forms and practise the shapes. If you need to erase anything, use the bread."

"The bread?" Emily was aghast.

"Did you think it was for tea?" Miss Carr said. "No, the bread's for rubbing out."

"Can't we have a little bite?" George asked.

"No, sir! Not even a nibble."

The studio was soon littered with charcoal-blackened crumbs and crusts. More bread was sliced and torn into chunks. "It's not for eating!" Miss Carr kept reminding them, but no one could resist.

Before Emily knew it, the class was over.

"Time for tea," Miss Carr announced as the kettle on the woodstove began to whistle. "Emily Too, you can pass the cookies."

After tea, Miss Carr collected everyone's class fees and put the coins into a boot. Then she hung the boot from a rafter by the door. "Next week," she said, "just pop the money into the boot when you arrive."

"What will you do with it all?" Jane asked.

Miss Carr smiled. "As soon as the boot's full, I'm going to London to study art."

"But you're already an artist," said Emily.

"Not yet!" she said. "I've got so much to learn."

"I don't understand," Jane said as they were walking home. "Being as old as Miss Carr and still wanting to learn things. I thought that when you grew up you knew everything."

"She doesn't act old," Emily remarked. "Not like a teacher. You should have seen her on the hill."

"She acts like one of us," said Jane. "I hope she never gets enough money to go away."

"Me too," said Emily. "I want to grow up and be just like her. And have a loft and invite my friends for tea. But I'll never be an artist."

"You might be," Jane said kindly.

"No, I don't think so. My raven looked more like a peacock. I'm hopeless! But it's such fun, I don't even care."

"I wish school were as much fun," said Jane.

Her words reminded Emily that Mei Yuk was starting school on Monday. What would it be like for her? Was she excited? She was bound to feel nervous, as Emily herself had felt on the way to art class. But hopefully, by the end of the day, things would turn out as well for Mei Yuk as they had for her.

Early Monday morning, Mei Yuk arrived at Emily's house ready for school. Her shoes were polished, her hands and face were scrubbed, her hair was shining, and she wore a crisp white pinafore. She smiled bravely at Bak Cheun as she said goodbye and clasped Emily's hand for the walk to school.

When they reached the school grounds, Alice called them over to join her and a group of friends. "This is Mei Yuk," she said. "She's going to be in our class."

The other girls exchanged glances. Some

smiled politely and said hello. A few walked away. Emily could hear them whispering and snickering behind her back. She could also hear the rude comments that some of the older boys were making, including Tom.

Mei Yuk noticed too. Although she couldn't understand what the boys were saying, there was no mistaking their tone. She stared at the ground and held Emily's hand more tightly.

It wasn't long before the principal, Miss Cameron, rang the bell and everyone went into the Assembly Hall for the morning exercises. Mei Yuk followed Emily's every move—standing for the singing of "O Canada" and "God Save the Queen," listening to the Bible reading, bowing her head for the saying of the Lord's Prayer.

After the assembly, the pupils filed off to their classrooms. Emily tried to ignore the looks cast in her and Mei Yuk's direction. Some were merely curious, but others were unfriendly, even hostile.

When they got to their classroom, Emily's teacher, Miss Wilson, greeted Mei Yuk warmly.

She gave her a slate and a chalk pencil and indicated to her that she could sit with Emily.

"I don't know how much you're able to understand," she said, "but your father has spoken to our principal and she has agreed to let you attend our class for a while, with other pupils your age, to see how you make out. I'm sure Emily will look after you."

Mei Yuk gave a small smile at the mention of Emily's name. As long as Emily was close by, she seemed to say, things would be fine.

The first hour passed quickly. Mei Yuk may not have understood much English, but she certainly understood numbers. She flew through the arithmetic questions that Miss Wilson put on the blackboard and ended up with more correct answers than many of her classmates.

When it was time for reading, Miss Wilson handed her an illustrated primer, the kind of book used by beginners.

"She should be in the primary school with the babies," one of the boys whispered. "She doesn't even know how to read."

Miss Wilson overheard. "I suppose you plunged straight into the third reader when you started school?"

"No, Miss," he replied.

"And since when have I allowed unkind remarks to be uttered in this classroom?"

"Never, Miss."

"Well, then? What do you have to say?"

"Sorry, Miss." But as soon as her back was turned, he looked over at Emily and glared.

Emily glared back. It wasn't *her* fault he had a big mouth.

Several of her classmates were still gawking, but Mei Yuk no longer seemed to notice. She held the primer as if she were handling a rare treasure. Then she placed it on the desk and gently ran her fingers over the cover.

"Open, close," Emily whispered, demonstrating with her reader.

Mei Yuk grinned. When she opened the primer and saw the first illustration, she gave an

audible gasp of pleasure. "Bird," she said, pointing. "Tree."

"Very good," said Miss Wilson. "Emily has
taught you well."

At recess, Emily and Mei Yuk once again found
themselves the centre of unwanted attention.
Several boys and girls were pulling faces and
calling them names.

"Just ignore them," said Alice. "Do you want to
play hopscotch?"

They showed her how to play and were happily
involved in the game when Tom swaggered over.

"You'd better clear off, Alice," he said.
"Remember what Ma said."

Alice threw her pebble and hopped onto the
squares without replying.

"I'll tell Ma," Tom persisted. "You'll get it when Pa comes home."

"Go away," said Emily. "She's not listening to you."

After taking her turn, however, Alice made an excuse and left to join her other friends.

Emily put on a brave face and tried not to care. Things would get better. Like Father always said, it was only a matter of time.

CHAPTER N.º 8

"You'd love my art class, Alice."

Three weeks had gone by. Alice had been away for most of it, stuck at home with a bad cold, and Emily had missed her. But now she was back at school. It was recess, and with Mei Yuk inside practising her printing, Emily and Alice were strolling about the playground arm in arm.

"It's such fun!" Emily continued. "Miss Carr sings out of tune and makes everyone laugh. There's a dog called Watch—remember, we saw him on the hill? And at the end of every class we have tea and cookies." She told Alice how shocked she'd been when she recognized Miss Carr, and how surprised she'd been to find out that George was taking lessons too.

"I heard about George," Alice remarked. "Tom won't have anything to do with him any more. He says he's a sissy, drawing and painting with girls."

"Well, it doesn't bother George. Wouldn't you like to take lessons? It might not be too late."

"I'd never be allowed," Alice said. "Ma knows all about Miss Carr. She says she's very odd. She goes on camping trips in the wilderness all by herself. And one day, Ma saw her out horseback riding—"

"What's wrong with that?"

"She wasn't riding sidesaddle, she was sitting astride, like a man! In long skirts! It's as bad as rolling down a hill. And a friend of Ma's saw her at a dance and said she just sat on the stairs and glowered. She's also bad-tempered—"

"She is not!"

"And she wears dowdy clothes and has no manners."

"That's not true!" Emily said hotly. "You shouldn't listen to gossip, Alice. Just because Miss Carr doesn't act like everybody else doesn't mean she's odd."

"Maybe you're right. Maybe it's *you* who's odd. You and that sissy, George."

"Oh, Alice!" Emily gave her a playful nudge, trying to lighten the mood. "Let's play the favourite game. You start."

"All right," said Alice. "And I'll be you. Favourite day? Saturday, because I won't have time to see Alice. I'll be too busy playing school with Mei Yuk in the morning and drawing with George in the afternoon."

"Alice—"

"Favourite subject? Art. Favourite pastime? Teaching Mei Yuk. Best friend? Mei Yuk."

"Alice, stop it! You know you're my best friend."

Alice let out a loud sigh. "I know. I'm just teasing. But honestly, Em, I never see you any more."

"Because you've been ill!"

"But before that." Alice pouted. "You're taking art lessons and spending all your spare time with Mei Yuk. It's just like the saying. Two's company, three's a crowd."

"You didn't think so last year when Florence was here," Emily reminded her. "Now you know how *I* felt."

"Yes, but that was different. Florence wasn't from China."

Emily groaned with frustration and switched to another topic. "Let's talk about the party. It's going to be this Friday. That is, if you're still coming."

"Of course!" Alice brightened. "I wouldn't miss a party, especially not a Jubilee."

By four o'clock on Friday afternoon, Emily had to face the fact that no one was coming to the

Beautiful Jade Jubilee. She had invited six girls from her class and all six had accepted. But no one had come. Not even Alice.

It was lucky that the party was supposed to be a surprise for Mei Yuk. She'd never have to know and be disappointed. Emily and her sisters taught her how to play pin the tail on the donkey and blindman's buff. Afterwards, they ate jam tarts and sipped raspberry cordial.

While they were waiting for Bak Cheun to fetch Mei Yuk, Emily showed her the drawings she'd done in her art class. To Emily's surprise, Mei Yuk admired them and asked if she might try.

"Sure," Emily said. She gave Mei Yuk some paper and charcoal, expecting her to copy some of Emily's sketches. Instead, Mei Yuk drew a river, some mountains, and a cluster of small huts.

"Home," Mei Yuk said. "China." With a few deft strokes she added chickens, dogs, water buffalo, and people.

Emily was impressed. "That's a beautiful picture," she said. "You can draw way better than

I can." She watched as Mei Yuk added more details to the scene, then asked, "Do you miss your home in China?"

"Miss?" Mei Yuk looked puzzled.

"Do you still feel lost?" Emily tried to explain. "Like in your nightmare?"

"No nightmare." Mei Yuk smiled. "Nightmare lost. You lost nightmare?" She gave Emily a hopeful look.

"Yes," Emily said. "The Door Guardians scared them away." It wasn't true, but she didn't want to hurt Mei Yuk's feelings.

When Bak Cheun arrived, Mei Yuk showed him her drawing, as well as the copybook Miss Wilson had given her. Mei Yuk knew her alphabet now, so she could practise printing words and simple sentences.

"Thank you, Em-ry," she said as she was leaving. "I am happy."

Emily smiled, warmed by the notion that she might have done a good job of oiling Mei Yuk's "wheel of life," at least for today. Maybe her mother's magazine was right, unselfishness *was* the root of perfect pleasure.

She was basking in the warm feeling when Alice unexpectedly came to the door.

"I'm sorry, Em," she said. There was a catch in her voice, and her eyes were red and swollen. "I can't come in. Ma told the other mothers that Mei Yuk was coming to the party. I didn't tell her. Tom did. And Ma told everyone that Mei Yuk was dirty and ill-mannered, and they're all signing a petition to ask the School Board to put her in a separate school because she has a bad influence on white children." She sniffed loudly and swallowed back a sob. "But that's not the worst of it."

Emily's stomach churned. Somehow she knew what was coming.

"Ma said that I'm not allowed to play with you, as long as you're friends with Mei Yuk. That you're becoming a bad influence, too. And not just because of Mei Yuk. It's also because of Miss Carr."

Emily was speechless. It was unfair, untrue, unkind, every "un" word she could think of. What was Alice asking of her? To choose between one friend and another? To give up her art lessons because of what some people thought about her teacher?

It wasn't so long ago that she'd wanted Alice to choose between her and Florence. Alice hadn't chosen; she'd wanted them all to be friends. Eventually the girls had worked things out themselves. But now, with parents involved, Emily would be forced to make a decision.

She swallowed hard. "I don't know what to say."

There was an awkward silence. Then they both spoke at once.

"Well . . ."

"I guess . . ."

"You first," said Alice.

"Well," Emily said, "I guess we'd better say goodbye."

Alice looked taken aback. "You mean you're not—?"

"No." Emily knew what Alice was expecting her to do. But she couldn't, not even for her best friend.

"Goodbye, then," Alice said sadly. She gave Emily a quick hug, then turned and walked away.

Unable to hold back the tears, Emily ran to her room and flung herself across the bed.

Her mother came in after her. "Emily, what is it?"

"Alice can't play with me any more," she sobbed. "Her mother—"

"Oh, dear. I know. Mrs. Kerr asked me to sign the petition too. Of course, I refused. I told her that Mei Yuk is a charming girl, clean, tidy, and diligent. I also told her that you're free to make your own decisions where friends are concerned, and that you're learning as much from Mei Yuk as Mei Yuk is learning from you."

This was a surprise. "What am I learning from her?" Emily asked. "I can't even speak her language."

"You're learning valuable lessons in becoming

a good citizen," Mother said. "You're growing up strong and noble and true to yourself."

"I don't want to be all that! I just want Alice to like me again."

"She still likes you," Mother said. She drew Emily close and stroked her hair. "Don't worry. Things will work out in time, you'll see."

"Nothing works out in time," Emily argued. "You said my nightmares would end with time and they didn't. They're getting worse."

"That's because the 24th of May is coming up," Mother said. "It's on everyone's mind, the anniversary of the disaster. But once that's over . . ." She gave Emily a hug. "I'm so proud of you. There isn't a single day that I don't thank God for your being here."

"But what should I do?" Emily said. "If Alice won't talk to me because of Mei Yuk—?"

"You'll know what to do. And remember, it's not what Alice wants, either. She's obeying her parents. As she should."

"Even when they're wrong?"

"Oh, Emily. That's one of the many things you learn when you're growing up. That, right or wrong, there are no easy answers."

CHAPTER N.º 9

"Where's Mei Yuk? She's always on time." Emily had been waiting anxiously for over twenty minutes for Mei Yuk to arrive so they could walk to school together. Was her friend ill? Was Bak Cheun unable to bring her? What if Mei Yuk had tried to come on her own and had got lost?

Another possibility came to mind. What if the School Board had accepted Mrs. Kerr's petition and told Mei Yuk she could no longer attend school?

"It's not that," Mother said. "I've learned that the School Board doesn't have the right to separate Chinese children from other children. And there's another thing you should know. Last week the Board asked the teachers for their opinion, and they praised Mei Yuk for her good behaviour and attitude."

"So where is she?" Emily continued to fret.

After another ten minutes had gone by, Mother said, "If you don't go now, you'll be late for school. You'll just have to leave without her."

Emily reluctantly agreed. But as she was setting off on her bicycle she thought, Why not go and look for Mei Yuk? I could bike at least as far as the James Bay Bridge and see if they're coming across. I'd still be on time for school.

When she reached the bridge, she stopped and looked. But there was no sign of Mei Yuk or her brother.

Something was wrong. Emily felt it in the pit of her stomach. There was only one thing to do—forget about school and keep going.

She was halfway across the bridge when she noticed a commotion on the beach. The tide was out, and the usual scavengers were on the mud flats, rummaging through cast-off boots, cooking pots, kettles, and the like. But the commotion was not coming from them. On the far shore, near the soap-works factory, a group of boys was chasing someone, yelling and throwing stones. Emily's heart clenched as she recognized Bak Cheun and, a little farther along, Mei Yuk.

A feeling of rage erupted inside. She pedalled furiously across the bridge and down the street. Then she dropped her bicycle at the factory and ran onto the shore.

By now, one of the boys had caught hold of Bak Cheun's pigtail and was laughing as Bak Cheun tried to fight him off. Mei Yuk had slipped and fallen in the mud, and the rest of the boys were swarming around her.

"You bullies!" Emily shrieked. "Leave them alone!"

The boys turned and glared. Tom was among them. He had Mei Yuk's copybook in his hand.

With a sneer at Emily, he hurled it into the factory sludge that spewed into the bay.

Emily glared back at the boys, her heart pounding. She was terrified that they might now turn on her. What could she do against five big boys? What could she say? "Leave Mei Yuk and her brother alone or I'll tell your parents"? Tom's parents wouldn't care. They didn't go as far as throwing stones, but their words and actions were every bit as hurtful.

Just then, one of the scavengers looked up from his rummaging. Seeing what was going on, he straightened up and came towards the boys. "Clear off, lads," he said gruffly. "You've had your fun."

His words prompted Emily into action. She pushed past the boys and helped Mei Yuk to her feet. Then she retrieved the copybook and wiped it off as best she could.

Tom and the others laughed unpleasantly as they swaggered off.

"You're a bunch of seagulls!" Emily hurled after them. "You think you're brave when you're in a

big mob." Turning to Mei Yuk, she said, "We can go to my house and get you cleaned up. You can wear one of my pinafores, and I've an extra pair of shoes. Don't worry about being late. Mother will write a note and explain everything."

"No," said Mei Yuk, reaching for her brother's hand. Her eyes welled up with tears.

Emily tried to reassure her. "It'll be better tomorrow. They won't bother you again."

"No," Mei Yuk repeated. "No school tomorrow. No school today. We go home now."

"But you can't!" Emily pleaded. "That's what they want."

Bak Cheun gave her a sombre look. "Every day is the same."

"What do you mean?"

"Same boy, other boy, always the same. Today, very bad."

"This happens every day?" A sob rose up in Emily's throat.

But how could she not have known? Memories of little things came flooding in. A torn page in

Mei Yuk's copybook, a bruise on her cheek . . . She'd dismissed them as the usual things that happen to children. She'd certainly had her fair share of bumps and bruises. But Mei Yuk had never said a word.

Emily fought back the urge to cry. "But Mei Yuk!" she pleaded. "You love school! Please don't quit now. You've worked so hard and learned so much."

"No," Mei Yuk insisted, wiping her eyes with the back of her hand. "No school. Sorry."

In her heart, Emily couldn't blame her. How could she encourage Mei Yuk to keep coming, knowing what she had to endure? At least there were only two weeks left before the holidays.

"I'll help you in the summer," she said. "And maybe in September . . ."

"Maybe." Mei Yuk gave her a small smile. Then she and Bak Cheun turned and walked away.

It was recess by the time Emily arrived at school.

"Why are you so late?" Alice asked.

Emily told her.

"Tom's a pig!" Alice said with disgust. "I hate him." She paused for a moment, and her expression brightened a bit. "So Mei Yuk isn't coming back to school?"

"You needn't sound so pleased," said Emily.

"I'm not. Not about that."

"What, then?"

"Well . . . now we can be friends again."

Exasperated with Alice and still upset by the morning's events, Emily threw up her hands and cried, "What do you mean, now? Nothing's changed! Mei Yuk is still my friend."

"But that's not fair to me!" Alice wailed. "It's not my fault you made friends with a Chinese girl."

"It's nobody's fault—" Emily was about to say more, but the ringing of the bell put an end to their discussion.

Once in the classroom, she gave Miss Wilson the note her mother had written, explaining Emily's lateness and Mei Yuk's absence.

"I'm sorry," her teacher said. "Do you think she might change her mind and come back?"

Emily shook her head sadly.

A few of her classmates asked about Mei Yuk, but she knew it was more out of curiosity than any real concern. She felt somewhat better when Miss Wilson gave her a primer to take to Mei Yuk, so she could keep up with her lessons. Beyond that, she could only hope that things would be better in the fall.

CHAPTER № 10

"Today I'd like you to draw whatever you please," Miss Carr said as she handed out sheets of paper. "Draw what you did this morning or last Sunday. Draw something you saw on your way to school. Or draw a nursery rhyme."

Emily and the others exchanged glances. So many choices! They never had to make choices like this in school.

"Help yourself to bread," Miss Carr continued. "You know what to do. And no nibbling!" She cast a stern look at her pupils, then turned and busied herself at her easel.

The pupils seized their chance and reached for the bread. Emily took a bite and almost choked. Some of the others coughed and gagged.

"It's full of salt!" Emily shrieked. "Miss Carr! You did it on purpose!"

Miss Carr's shoulders were shaking with laughter, and when she turned around she had a smug look on her face. "I can't have you eating all the erasers, can I? Now, on with your drawings."

"I think I'll draw a nursery rhyme," said Jane. "But, Miss Carr, which one should it be?"

"Whatever takes your fancy. 'Humpty-Dumpty.' 'Jack Be Nimble.' 'London Bridge Is Falling Down.' And don't worry if it doesn't look perfect. Be free and fantastical. Let your imagination soar."

Emily decided to draw "London Bridge." But it wasn't long before she realized that she wasn't drawing the bridge from her picture book. Instead she was drawing Point Ellice Bridge. The centre span had collapsed, and the streetcar was lying at the bottom of the Gorge. People were trapped inside.

Her heart thudded painfully. The nightmare was coming out on the page. She tightened her grip on the charcoal, afraid to continue but unable to stop. She now found herself drawing Florence and the other girl, the one being dragged to the bottom.

This is me . . . Her breath came in ragged gasps. The wide-open eyes. The mouth, a large O. A silent scream . . .

She flung down the charcoal and buried her face in her hands. The room was unusually quiet. Had she screamed out loud?

She felt a hand on her shoulder. "Were you there, Emily Too?" Miss Carr asked gently.

Emily nodded, struggling to hold back the tears. "I have this nightmare . . ."

"And now you've captured it on paper. That's a good place for it, don't you think?" Miss Carr gave her an encouraging smile. "Maybe it won't bother you again."

Emily had never thought of that. If the nightmare were on the page and not in her head . . .

An idea came to her. "I can change it," she said. She erased the two girls and started again. This time, the Emily in the picture was holding Florence's hand and pulling her up to the surface. Emily put smiles on their faces. And then, to make the picture complete, she added Alice.

When she got home, Emily looked at the Door Guardians and came up with another idea. She folded her drawing and tucked it under her pillow, hoping that the true picture would scare away the images in her nightmare. This, after all, was how things had turned out. Emily, Florence, and Alice—all three of them, safe and sound.

On fine days, Miss Carr held her classes outdoors. Accompanied by Watch, the retriever, the whole group set off for the park or the beach armed with easels, folding camp stools, paper, and watercolour boxes.

They could draw or paint whatever they liked—wildflowers, stunted oak trees, the rocky cliffs hugging the sea, or the Olympic Mountains floating in a mist across the strait.

Emily loved these outings. But on this particular day she was feeling less happy than usual. She missed seeing Mei Yuk at school, and her friendship with Alice was not as close as it had been. The fact that this was the last art class of the season only added to her glumness.

At least they were going to Beacon Hill. When the class reached the hillside, Emily settled in the long grass amid the wildflowers and viewed her surroundings.

Miss Carr set up her easel beside her. "What a splendid day," she said cheerfully.

Emily agreed. The day suddenly seemed much brighter with Miss Carr at her side.

"What will you paint today, Emily Too?" her teacher asked.

"Camas lilies," said Emily. "I love the colour." She was becoming quite adept at using her watercolours, and finding the right mix of purple and blue for the camas would be a challenge.

"That'll keep you out of mischief," Miss Carr quipped.

They painted in silence for a while. Then, to make conversation, Emily asked, "What was your favourite place when you were a little girl?"

"Beacon Hill Park," Miss Carr replied.

"Mine too!" said Emily. "What was your favourite thing to do?"

"You mean besides rolling down the hill? I liked to sit on big wooden fences and watch the birds. I liked seeing what the birds were doing."

"I do too!" Emily grinned. They had three things in common! Thinking back to her teacher's earlier remark, she asked, "Did you ever get into mischief?" She immediately wanted to take back the question. Imagine, asking a grown-up that sort of thing! Her mother would be horrified if she knew.

But Miss Carr only laughed. "Oh, yes! One day I took a sick-looking hen into somebody's parlour and doctored it with castor oil. It recovered right on the spot, all over the carpet. And I used to serenade the cow at the top of my lungs. My sisters said the neighbours complained, but I didn't care. I'm still that way, you know. I don't give a hoot what other people think."

Right then and there, Emily decided that she wouldn't give a hoot either. Starting with Alice. She wouldn't worry about their friendship anymore. She just wouldn't care.

CHAPTER N.º 11

By the middle of June, Victoria was blossoming with signs of the Diamond Jubilee. Streets, buildings, carriages—the entire city was bedecked with flags and bunting, floral displays, crowns of evergreens, and, above all, pictures of Queen Victoria. Stores had already sold out of the coveted Jubilee brooches, and anyone wanting to buy red, white, or blue cotton was out of luck.

The schools joined in the decorating frenzy, and South Park was no exception. Seated in the Assembly Hall for the year-end awards ceremony,

Emily proudly took in her school's contribution—a huge portrait of Her Majesty surrounded by evergreen boughs and flanked with Canadian ensigns and Union Jacks.

In spite of the festive occasion, she wished that the afternoon would end. Pupils in each class were receiving prizes for attendance, punctuality, deportment, diligence, arithmetic, geography, spelling, writing . . . on and on it went. Emily yawned. She'd won ribbons for races, but she'd never won a prize for schoolwork. Nor did she expect to. Bored and discouraged, she began to count the flags.

A burst of applause drew her attention back to the ceremony. Another diligent pupil . . .

That was the prize Mei Yuk deserved. A prize for diligence and perseverance. Emily knew that Miss Wilson felt the same way. Only that morning her teacher had spoken about Mei Yuk and praised her attitude. She had even told the class they could all take a page out of Mei Yuk's book.

At the front of the hall, Miss Cameron was speaking at the podium. "This year, for the first time, we have a new prize. A book—awarded to the most altruistic pupil in each class."

Altruistic? Emily frowned. What did that mean?

"The books were given by an anonymous friend," Miss Cameron continued. "Someone who wishes to recognize the spirit that prompts one to stop the race for his own advancement, in order to give another a helping hand. Our first winner, in the Fifth Division . . ."

Emily's attention went back to the flags.

"Now we come to the Fourth Division," Miss Cameron was saying. "And the winner is . . . Emily Murdoch!"

At first Emily thought she was hearing things. But when Miss Wilson smiled and said, "Go on! Up you go!" she realized that it was true.

She rose shakily, her face burning with a mixture of excitement and nervousness. The platform seemed so far away. Please don't let me trip, she prayed. Not in front of the whole school!

When she reached the platform, Miss Cameron shook her hand and presented her with her prize. "In two days we celebrate Queen Victoria's Diamond Jubilee," she said. "I can think of no better way to honour Her Majesty than to recognize those who have embraced the feeling of brotherhood and altruism to an outstanding degree. Congratulations, Emily. Your prize is well deserved."

"Miss Cameron was wrong. I *don't* deserve it," Emily said at supper that night. "I helped Mei Yuk with her English, but it wasn't enough. All those times, when she was coming to school and getting bullied—I didn't help her with that. And then she gave up."

"You did your best," Mother said. "There are some battles that are too big for one little girl to take on . . . even if she is very brave and determined."

"And artistic," said Amelia.

"You mean *altruistic,*" Jane said. "Isn't that right, Em?"

Emily nodded. "I looked it up. It means being unselfish and considering the welfare of others. I just wish . . ."

"We're proud of you," Father said. "You made a start, and Mei Yuk did, too. That's what's important."

"I'll share my book with her," said Emily. "She can still come here in the summer, can't she?"

"Of course," Mother said. "Mei Yuk will always be welcome here."

On the day of the Jubilee, Emily and her family joined thousands of others on Beacon Hill to take part in an open-air service of thanksgiving. Everyone was dressed up to display their patriotism. White frocks with red and blue sashes, Jubilee brooches, Union Jack neckties, and tricolour hatbands were the order of the day.

The area surrounding the hill had been transformed. Off to the side, a tent city had been set up for visiting soldiers. And at the base of the hill, directly below where Emily and her family were sitting, a pulpit had been erected.

"It's a church with a blue-sky roof," Emily remarked. There would be no rolling down the hill today.

Soon the parade came into view. A grand marshal on a spirited white horse led the way, followed by societies of Englishmen, Irishmen, Scotsmen, native-born Canadians, and pioneers. They marched proudly into the square surrounding the pulpit.

Emily recognized Mr. Kerr among the Sons of Englishmen. She wished that he'd trip and disgrace himself. It would serve him right. Then she remembered that she was in church, in a way, and immediately asked God to forgive her uncharitable thoughts.

Once the marchers and special guests had been seated, the service began. The band played the opening hymn, "All People that on Earth do Dwell," and thousands of voices joined in song. Emily sang out the hymn, hoping that Mr. Kerr and Tom and everyone else would take the words to heart. The hymn meant *all* people. Not just white people.

She thought about this during the sermon and wondered why things had to be so difficult. Getting older didn't seem to change anything. Grown-up Mr. Kerr had the same mean attitude as Tom. He likely encouraged Tom to treat the Chinese badly.

The shrill cry of a bugle interrupted her thoughts and turned her attention to the flagstaff crowning Beacon Hill. As the Royal Standard was hoisted to the top, the band struck up and people raised their voices in the singing of "God Save the Queen."

At the end of the anthem, another minister took his place at the podium. *Another* sermon. Emily groaned silently and tried not to fidget.

"With profound reverence," he began, "do we in this part of the great British Empire join in the thanks which circle the globe today, the sixtieth anniversary of our beloved Queen's reign. Only those who lived before her reign can fully realize the contrast between what was and what is, from merciless oppression and greed to education for the poor and care for the afflicted. These are but some of the precious jewels which by the grace of God adorn Victoria's crown . . ."

Emily's attention wavered. She scanned the crowd, searching for familiar faces, and spotted a woman in a black dress completely covered with little Union Jacks. It turned out to be Mrs. Kerr, and Alice was sitting beside her.

Emily hadn't seen Alice since the end of school. She willed her friend to turn around so she could wave or smile, but Alice seemed intent on listening to the sermon.

Seeing Alice made Emily wonder if she, too, would be attending the military review in Esquimalt the next day. Emily was dreading it. For the first time since the disaster, she would have to go across the Point Ellice Bridge. Her nightmares had miraculously stopped since she'd drawn the picture and placed it under her pillow, but the fear of crossing the bridge remained.

"Look, Em," Amelia whispered beside her. "I'm blowing up my balloon."

"Amelia!" Emily was horrified. She hoped her parents hadn't noticed. People had brought balloons to the service, but you didn't blow them up during the sermon.

The balloon was getting bigger and Amelia was almost out of breath. "Let me tie it," said Emily. She did so, and was about to hand it back when she saw Alice glancing her way. Momentarily distracted, she let go of the balloon.

At the same time, the minister concluded his sermon. Noting this, and seeing the balloon floating overhead, many people took it as a signal to release theirs.

"You lost my balloon!" Amelia sniffed.

"But look what I started!" Emily gazed up at the flurry of red, white, and blue soaring above the hillside. It was almost like an offering. She sent a prayer along with it—that tomorrow she would safely cross over the bridge.

"I can do it, I can do it . . ." Emily chanted the words as she took a seat in the crowded streetcar. She'd insisted on sitting on the right-hand side, as if it would once again be lucky. She also insisted that Father open the window.

She remained calm during the ride through town, but as the streetcar rolled onto the bridge she clenched her fists and squeezed her eyes shut. "I can do it . . ."

Father tried to reassure her by saying that lightning never struck the same spot twice. But Emily knew it wasn't true. Three years before the disaster, on the same 24th of May holiday, the same bridge had sagged under the weight of the very same car. It was only luck that had saved the passengers that day. Would today be a lucky day?

"Don't worry, dear," Mother said. "It's a brand-new bridge. It's built to carry heavy loads."

"I know," said Emily, "but I can't help thinking . . ."

Were they almost across? She risked a peek. Directly below, the waters of the Gorge glinted in the sunlight. She covered her eyes as a knot of fear rose up in her throat. She felt trapped inside her nightmare, unable to breathe. If only she'd thought to bring her drawing . . .

But she could draw it in her mind. Three girls smiling on the surface of the water. That was the truth. Her nightmare was only a might-have-been.

The clanging of the bell made her risk another peek. "We're back on land!" she exclaimed. "We really made it across?"

"Indeed we did," Father said.

"We still have to go back," she said anxiously.

"Yes, but let's cross that bridge when we come to it. All right? Put it out of your mind and enjoy the day."

Emily promised to try.

The grounds were packed by the time they reached Macaulay Point, but Father managed to find a spot that afforded a good view of the troops.

"When does the *jam battle* start?" Amelia asked.

"It's *sham* battle," Emily said. "Don't you remember? And there isn't a battle this time. It's only a review."

"There's marching and big guns going off," said Jane.

"Big guns?"

"Yes, but they're fired into the air and nobody gets hurt."

"Except when little girls ask too many questions," Emily said. "Then they bring out the cannons—" She broke off, leaving the sentence unfinished. "There's Alice!"

Alice was standing with her mother a short distance away. She must have come across the bridge too. Had it been as difficult for her? Emily felt a welling up inside. In spite of her determination not to give a hoot, as Miss Carr put it, she couldn't help but care. She and Alice had gone through the same terrifying experience and shared a bond too powerful to break. She had to smooth things over.

She thought for a moment and came up with an idea. After a few words to her parents, she picked her way through the crowd to talk to Alice.

Alice smiled when she saw her. "Hello, Emily," she said. "Congratulations on your prize. You deserved it."

"Thank you," Emily said. Then, "Alice, I was wondering . . ." She glanced nervously at Mrs. Kerr, took a deep breath, and plunged ahead.

"Would you like to come to the Illuminations with us tonight?"

Alice's face lit up. "May I?" she asked her mother.

Before Mrs. Kerr could reply, Emily added, "Mei Yuk's coming, too."

Mrs. Kerr bristled. "I'm surprised that you would ask, Emily."

"I asked because it's a special celebration and I want to share it. Alice is my best friend. But Mei Yuk is my friend, too, and I won't choose between them." She turned to Alice. "I wanted you to know that. I guess the rest is up to you."

As Alice was about to speak, a firing of guns signalled the start of the review.

"I'd better go back to my parents," Emily said. "Goodbye, Alice."

She hadn't gone far when Alice caught up. "Here," she said. She removed her Jubilee brooch and pressed it into Emily's hand. "Give this to Mei Yuk and tell her I'm sorry. Maybe one day . . ."

"I hope so," Emily said, and gave her a hug.

CHAPTER N°. 12

"Fire!" Mei Yuk exclaimed. Her face shone in the night.

Emily nodded excitedly.

They were standing on the summit of Beacon Hill and the enormous beacon fires had just been set ablaze. A fiery chain encircled the city, from Race Rocks in the west to Oak Bay in the east. And that wasn't all. Rockets and Roman candles were exploding in the sky, in showers of red, white, and blue.

"Will they see us from across the strait?" Emily wondered. The American side looked so close.

"They'll certainly see the beacons," her father said. "And to think that this is happening in every dominion that flies the British flag."

"The whole world is lit up," said Emily.

"Not the *whole* world," Jane argued.

"Well, almost. Miss Wilson told us that Queen Victoria rules 11 million square miles of land and 400 million people."

"How does she do that?" asked Amelia.

Emily shrugged. "I guess queens just know about that sort of thing."

After the fireworks display was over, they set off for the Inner Harbour to see the Illuminations, centred around the newly completed parliament buildings.

Emily held her breath in awe. She had often walked past the new parliament buildings but had never seen them like this. The entire design was traced with lights, from the basement to the tip of the dome. Lights streamed from every window. Above the main entrance, a royal crown glowed in coloured fire. On top of the dome, the gold statue of Captain Vancouver glittered with light, and the torch in his hand shone like a star.

Mei Yuk gasped in wonder.

"It's a fairyland," Emily sighed. "It's like magic."

"Magic," Mei Yuk repeated, savouring the word. "Magic."

Emily gazed at the lights, spellbound. She couldn't help but remember the Illuminations held during the previous year—the parade of boats trailing along the Gorge Waterway, people standing on the Point Ellice Bridge singing "God Save the Queen" . . . How happy she'd been that night. Yet within twenty-four hours, disaster had struck.

What would the next twenty-four hours bring? The next month? The next year?

One thing was certain. The memory of the disaster no longer filled her with dread. She had crossed over the bridge, twice in one day. It was bound to be easier the next time.

As for her friendship with Alice, it was up to Alice to make the next move. And whatever

Alice decided . . . Emily gave a determined smile and said to herself, I'll just cross that bridge when I come to it.

BOOK FOUR

Summer of Gold

CHAPTER N° 1

"Summer holidays!" Emily sang the words out loud. She'd left her house a few minutes earlier and was now biking along Dallas Road with the sea to her right, Beacon Hill to her left, the wind at her back, and a fine morning stretching ahead.

She swerved to avoid a pothole, narrowly missed another and, ringing her bicycle bell, flew past a horse-drawn carriage to escape the dust and dried manure kicked up by the horses' hooves. Beyond the carriage, the road was clear and the air held nothing but the scent of wild roses and the salty tang of the sea.

She kept to the road until she came to a grassy field overlooking the strait. Ignoring the bumps, she rode straight across the field to the edge of the cliff and dismounted. She left her bicycle in a thicket of rose bushes and clambered down the steep path to the beach.

Two months of holidays! After the excitement of Queen Victoria's Diamond Jubilee, Emily was afraid that the summer might be boring. She was also saddened by the possibility that she and her best friend, Alice, might not be able to see each other until they went back to school in September.

But today Emily was optimistic. She had other good friends, like Hing's daughter, Mei Yuk, and George Walsh. She had her sisters, Jane and Amelia, and her bicycle, and as of this morning, she had a plan—to go places where she might see Alice by chance. They both had bicycles, and they liked the same places. It was such a simple and obvious plan that she couldn't imagine why she hadn't thought of it sooner.

When she reached the bottom of the path, she surveyed the empty beach with high hopes. If Alice *were* to show up on a beach, this would be the one. They'd spent hours here in the past, hunting for treasures, building forts out of driftwood, splashing in the cold water, paddling on logs. George had often joined them, along with Alice's brother, Tom.

Emily grimaced at the thought of Tom. He'd always been a bit of a rascal, but not the bully he was now—picking on Mei Yuk and her brothers, sneering at Emily, making rude comments. Thank goodness *he* wasn't on the beach. Her morning would've been ruined if he had been.

She sat on a log and opened her sketchbook, pleased that she'd brought it along. She needed the practice. Besides, sketching on a beach was the very thing that Emily Carr, her art teacher, liked to do.

Pencil poised, she looked about for something to draw. Sandpipers running along the shore? The rocky outcrop? The steamship crossing the strait, with the mountains in the background? She'd sketched the mountains many times before, but why not? The ship would be a challenge. Recalling Miss Carr's words about shape and form, she began.

Several sketches later, and with still no sign of Alice, Emily closed her sketchbook and set off to do some beachcombing. She was strolling along, pausing now and then to pocket a smooth stone or a seashell, when she saw a mob of crows and seagulls swooping over something on the beach. From a distance, it looked like a bundle of dark clothing. But as she got closer, she saw that it was a dog.

A dead dog.

Her heart gave a turn. How long had the poor thing been lying there? His fur was still wet. Had the tide washed him in? Had he made it to shore on his own, only to give up at the end?

He'd been a fine-looking dog—medium in size, black with a white chest and muzzle, tan markings on his paws, a long tail, and pointed ears. But he was so thin! His ribs—

"Oh!" Emily started, wide-eyed with shock. The dog's chest was moving. His tail twitched. A tremor passed through his body. "You're alive!" Emily gasped. "It's a miracle!"

The dog made a horrible retching sound and struggled to his feet. Shaking uncontrollably, he heaved up buckets of seawater until finally, spent and exhausted, he collapsed again.

"Don't give up now!" Emily cried in alarm.

He whimpered at the sound of her voice and made a feeble attempt to wag his tail. Another tremor passed through him.

Emily leaned over and felt his side. In spite of the sunshine, he was freezing. And no wonder— the waters in the strait never warmed up, not even in the summer.

She took off her pinafore, wrapped it around the dog, and began to rub him down. "You must be a strong swimmer," she said. "As strong as Samson in the Bible story, only Samson wasn't a dog. I think that's what I'll call you. Samson, but Sam for short. Do you like that name?"

The dog gave another whimper, more like a sigh. He was still shivering.

"There, there, Sam," Emily murmured. "I'll take care of you."

First, she had to get him home. The nearest path to the top of the cliffs was only a few yards away. It was longer than the path she'd come down on, but since it wasn't as steep, she knew it would be an easier climb.

She picked Sam up and held him against her chest. He was as light as a rag doll but so cold that she too began to shiver.

But not for long! By the time she reached the road, she was drenched with sweat. With every step, Sam had grown heavier. Now he was starting to wheeze. "Easy, boy," she soothed. "We're almost there …"

Almost? Her house was still three long blocks away. She'd never make it. She'd have to stop somewhere and rest, or leave Sam and run home to get her mother.

Just then, she heard the Beacon Hill streetcar

clang to a stop behind her. As luck would have it, a familiar Scottish voice called out, "Hello, Emily! Need a hand?"

She turned and saw her neighbour stepping off the platform. "Mr. Sinclair! Am I glad to see you!"

He caught up to her and gently lifted Sam into his arms. "You're about done in, lass," he said. "You *and* the dog."

"Isn't he beautiful? I'm calling him Sam. I found him on the beach." She let Mr. Sinclair carry Sam until they reached her house, then insisted she could manage on her own. "I can't wait to show everyone," she said, and thanked him again.

Her sisters had spotted her from an upstairs window and came running outside, shrieking with delight.

"A dog! Emily's got a dog!"

"Where did you get him? Why's he shivering?"

"Mother, hurry! Emily's got a dog!"

"How come you're carrying him?"

"What's his name?"

"His name's Sam," Emily told them. "And you have to speak quietly. You're scaring him."

Mother met them on the back verandah. "Oh, Emily. Look at you. And this poor creature …"

"I'm calling him Sam."

"Well, Sam needs some attention and you need dry clothes. Away you go—and mind you have a good wash."

Emily reluctantly left Sam in the kitchen and did as she was told. A short time later, she came back and found him lying by the wood stove, wrapped in warm blankets and sleeping soundly.

Jane and Amelia were watching over him. "He drank some water," Jane reported. "And a bit of beef broth."

"Mother told us to pat him, to move his blood," said Amelia.

Emily smiled. "Doesn't he look contented? At first, I thought he was dead. But then he came to life before my very eyes." She told them the story, then bent down and planted a kiss on Sam's white muzzle. "I love him already."

"I know, dear," said Mother. "But don't get your hopes up."

"What? I can keep him, can't I?"

"Not if he belongs to someone else. He may have been trying to get home, you know. In any case, we'll see what your father has to say."

CHAPTER N.º 2

The possibility that Sam could be someone else's dog hadn't occurred to Emily, and she quickly put the thought from her mind. She kept herself busy while waiting for her father by washing the lunch dishes, pulling carrots from the garden, and helping Jane shell some green peas. She watered the garden, too, using the outside pump to fill one watering can after another.

Every few minutes, she went inside to check on Sam. Was he awake or asleep? Was he warm enough? Did he have enough water? Had he drunk more broth?

By late afternoon, he was beginning to stir. Emily mashed up some leftover beef stew and fed him a small amount. "Good dog," she said. "This will fatten you up."

He wagged his tail and took a few shaky steps around the kitchen, exploring the various nooks and corners before returning to his spot by the stove.

Emily kneeled beside him, stroking his head. If she biked to the James Bay Bridge and met her father on his way home from work, they could walk back together and she could tell him all about Sam. So by the time—

All at once she remembered. "My bicycle! I left it on the cliff!"

"Quick, then!" Mother said. "Go back and get it."

Emily rushed off in a flap. How careless! She was everything a girl who wanted a dog should *not* be—forgetful, absent-minded, scatterbrained— what would Father say now? She couldn't have ridden her bicycle with Sam, but she should have gone right back to get it. And her sketch-book! She'd forgotten that, too.

At least she remembered where she'd left her bicycle. She headed straight for the rose thicket—but the bicycle was gone. She searched all around the cliff, the path, and finally, the beach. Her sketchbook was still on the log. But there was no sign of her bicycle.

She choked back a sob. Who would take a girl's bicycle? Especially one with faded ribbons tied to the spokes?

She trudged home tearfully, dreading the moment she would have to face her father.

He was home when she arrived. He listened to her story and agreed that she'd been careless but understandably so, given her concern about the dog. He also pointed out that the bicycle may well have gone missing while she was still on the beach.

He wrote out a description, asked Emily for more details about where and when she'd last seen the bicycle, and left for town. He was going straight to the police station to file a report.

He returned a short time later and announced that he'd also stopped by the newspaper office and placed an ad about the dog. "If no one claims him by the end of the week," he said, "Sam can stay. But don't count your bridges."

"Chickens!" Amelia corrected. "Don't count your chickens before they're hatched."

"Quite so. As long as you all understand and don't get too attached to the dog."

"I already am," said Emily.

Her father wagged a finger in her direction. "As long as you realize that someone might be missing Sam as much as you are missing your bicycle. Meanwhile, I'm going to ask Dr. Murphy to drop by and have a look."

"He's a horse doctor!" Jane blurted.

"A veterinarian treats all animals, Jane. He'll be able—"

"Worms, too?" Amelia wondered. "And slugs?"

"They're not animals," said Jane.

"Are too."

"Are not!"

"Are too! And cows."

"Girls!" Father silenced them with a look. "Dr. Murphy will decide if Sam's basically healthy or if he needs any special treatment. Now, after walking back and forth to town three times within the last hour, I'm ready for my dinner."

Emily waited anxiously for the week to pass, fearing that a stranger might show up at any moment to take back the dog. Happily, no one came. At the end of the week, Sam was welcomed as an official member of the Murdoch family.

Dr. Murphy had told them that Sam was about two years old and most likely a mix of border collie and Labrador, with a fair bit of something else. He couldn't say how the dog had ended up in the water. Sam's previous owner might have gone off in a boat and left him behind. Maybe the dog had tried to follow. Maybe there'd been a boating accident. Or maybe the owner had purposely dumped Sam overboard to be rid of him. Sadly, people did take such actions. The fact that Sam had survived, in spite of his undernourished condition, showed great strength, endurance, and determination.

Before leaving, Dr. Murphy had praised Emily for being such a fine judge of canine character.

"She was born in the Year of the Dog," Jane had remarked, as if that explained everything.

Over the next few weeks, Sam's health slowly improved. His nose stayed cold and moist, his coat began to shine, and his eyes became bright and alert. On daily walks to Beacon Hill Park, Emily and her sisters taught him to sit, stay, and heel. Later, they taught him to fetch, to shake a paw, and to say *please*.

Emily refused to let Jane teach him to play dead, not after he'd had such a near-death experience. And as for dressing him up, she was furious when she discovered Sam wearing Amelia's Sunday bonnet and an apron. "How could you, Amelia?" she fumed. "He's not a doll! See how he's hanging his head? He's embarrassed!"

"He likes it," Amelia pouted.

"Well, it's not dignified for a canine. So don't do it again."

"Bossy," Amelia muttered and stuck out her tongue.

Sam learned quickly. Emily liked to think it was all her doing, but Sam may well have been taught the basics by someone in his former home. And she had to give her family some credit. It took a few harsh words from Mother and Father before Sam stopped rolling in the flower beds and burying bones in the vegetable garden.

CHAPTER N.º 3

"What a handsome dog! So well behaved and obedient!"

Emily smiled at the passersby as she led Sam through the busy section of town. Although she wasn't solely responsible for his behaviour, she basked in the praise.

She was on her way to Chinatown for her weekly visit with Mei Yuk and, for the first time, she was taking Sam. She'd tied a leash to his collar to make sure he didn't run off, and he was behaving admirably. It was a wonder, with so many distractions. People, horses, dogs, carriages, wagons, streetcars, a herd of cattle being driven down to the wharf—the noise and traffic were enough to distract anyone.

And the smells! Sam tried to stop at the butcher's shop, where sides of beef and strings of pork sausage hung temptingly over the board-walk, but Emily was firm. "Come, Sam," she said. "We'll stop for a bone on the way back."

She, too, was finding it hard not to be distracted. She hadn't walked to Chinatown in a long time, and it seemed much farther than when she'd taken her bicycle. She'd been so happy with Sam she hadn't really missed her bicycle, not *terribly*, but now she looked at bicycles in the street, hoping she might spot her own. What could have happened to it? Would she ever get it back? Sam would love running alongside as she biked to the park or to the waterfront or through town.

At last, they reached Chinatown. Emily turned down a brick alley, crossed a narrow lane, and found herself in the courtyard behind Hing's restaurant. "Mei Yuk!" she called, seeing her friend through the kitchen window. "Come and meet Sam."

Mei Yuk gave a cheerful wave and hurried outside, followed by her father.

"You can pet him if you like," said Emily. "He's very friendly."

Mei Yuk crouched down and reached out her hand. Sam gave it a sniff and, smelling something tasty, began to lick her fingers.

Hing laughed. "He like Hing special chicken, same as Em-ry."

"We taught him some tricks," Emily said. "Watch." She put Sam through his paces, ending with, "Sam, lie down."

He yawned, circled three times, and obeyed.

"May I leave him out here while we have our English lesson?" Emily asked.

"No, we do the lesson here," Mei Yuk said. "Please, Father? Too hot inside."

Hing agreed, and with his help they pulled together some crates and boards to make a couple of desks.

While Mei Yuk was upstairs gathering her books, Emily went into the kitchen to say hello to Mei Yuk's mother and brothers. She came out a short time later with a bowl of water and a big juicy bone. "Say *please,*" she said.

At that moment, Mei Yuk appeared. "Remember, Em-ry?" she laughed. "First lesson. Mei Yuk, sit. Mei Yuk, stand. Now, Sam, sit. Sam, stand. Sam, say *please!*"

Emily joined in the laughter, remembering how difficult their first lesson had been and how much Mei Yuk had learned since then. She could draw, too, even without taking art lessons.

That gave Emily an idea. She opened her satchel and took out her sketchbook. "Mei Yuk, would you draw me a picture of Sam? I tried, but you're much better."

"Thank you," Mei Yuk said modestly. She observed Sam stretched out on the cobblestones, gnawing on his bone. With a few bold strokes and a little shading, she managed to capture what Emily called "the essence of his canine character."

To finish, Mei Yuk took a red pencil from her box and printed *Emily Dog Sam* at the top of the page. "Red is for good luck," she said.

Emily hugged her friend. She felt that she ought to mention the apostrophe *s* that Mei Yuk had left out, but since it was summer and she wasn't a real teacher anyway, she let it go.

The lesson passed quickly with a bit of reading, some printing, and an easy spelling test.

As Emily was getting ready to leave, Hing came out to say goodbye. "Be careful," he said. "Watch Sam. Many people want dog today."

"Why?" Emily was puzzled.

"For new Gold Mountain." Before he could go on, a startled cry came from the kitchen, followed by a clatter of pots and a hiss of steam. "Aie, Bak Cheun!" He rushed inside, uttering a string of words that Emily didn't understand.

"Bak Cheun learn to cook," Mei Yuk said sympathetically. "He make … mistake?"

"Mistakes," Emily corrected. "More than one."

Mei Yuk nodded. "Many mistakes. Like me, in spelling."

"No, Mei Yuk! You almost had a perfect score today. Next week, you'll do even better."

With that, Emily left for home.

By now it was late afternoon, and the streets were busier than ever. People were gathering on the boardwalks and in shop doorways, talking with an unusual amount of fervour.

"Have you heard …?"

"… leaving first thing tomorrow."

"Terrible shame to miss it … you know what they say about the early bird …"

"… a bonanza!"

Block after block, Emily heard snippets of similar conversations. Something was afoot. There was a feeling of celebration, as if it were Christmas, the Diamond Jubilee, and the 24th of May all rolled into one. Why, on an ordinary Tuesday?

She had just passed the butcher's shop when she spotted Mr. Sinclair across the street. He was talking to a group of men, his face flushed with excitement. *He'd* tell her what was going on.

She stopped on the edge of the boardwalk, waited for a streetcar to pass, and stepped onto the street. "Come, Sam. Heel!" She tugged on his leash, but it came loose in her hand and Sam bounded away. "Sam!" she yelled anxiously. He couldn't go far, but with so many people around, anything might happen.

She turned to follow Sam and spotted him at once. The rascal! He was sitting outside the butcher's shop, unabashedly wagging his tail as a bearded stranger fed him sausages.

"Sam, come here!" Emily commanded.

He gave her a guilty look, gulped down another sausage, and slunk towards her, tail between his legs.

"Bad dog!" she said, retying the leash to his collar. "You know you're to come when you're called."

"Nice dog you got there," the sausage man remarked. "Can he pull a sled?"

The question took Emily by surprise. "Probably! But only in the winter."

"Too bad," he said. "I can't wait that long."

Emily frowned but didn't stop to ask what he meant. Why would he care if Sam could pull a sled? And what was the big hurry? His comments were as strange as Hing's remark about Gold Mountain. What was *that* supposed to mean? She knew that the Chinese had once used the expression to describe British Columbia as a land of golden opportunities. Hing had been one of thousands who'd come to work on the railway many years ago, but whose dreams of wealth had not come true. Did a new Gold Mountain mean another railway was being built? If so, why would people want a dog?

At dinner that evening, Emily talked about her day and asked her father if he'd noticed anything unusual in town.

"I did, as a matter of fact," he said. "And I'll tell you why. Some people came up from Seattle this afternoon with word of a gold discovery. What Hing probably meant by 'Gold Mountain' was that a lot of people will put their dreams into something that won't come true. You know how it is. Word spreads and the story gets bigger and people get carried away."

"Like making a mole out of a molehill," said Amelia.

"No, silly," Jane laughed. "It's a *mountain* out of a molehill."

"Quite so," said Father. "It could be nothing at all."

He couldn't have been more wrong.

CHAPTER N⁰ 4

Seattle Is Wild! Rush for the Gold!

The newspaper headlines made it official. By the following day, Victoria was as wild as Seattle. The ripple of excitement that Emily had noticed had swollen into a frenzy. Newsboys, clerks, shopkeepers, hack drivers, streetcar conductors, friends, neighbours—everyone had something to say. After all, it was no ordinary discovery. It was a bonanza—an exceptionally large and rich discovery of gold.

"I'll never get my shopping done," Emily's mother complained. She and the girls had taken the streetcar to town, but every time they turned around, they were stopped by someone wanting to spread the news.

Mr. Saunders, the butcher, was the latest to hold them up. "Have you heard?" he asked. "Three prospectors up in the Yukon were panning for gold on a little creek and now they're million-aires. Arrived in Seattle two days ago with their baggage so full of nuggets they could hardly lug it off the ship."

And so it went, in one shop after another.

"… picking up nuggets by the handful!"

"Nuggets the size of potatoes …"

"When's the next ship heading north? Where can I buy a ticket?"

"Emily!" George waved from a newsstand across the street and ran over to join her. "Have you heard the news? I read in the paper that a prospector found a slab of gold as thick as a slice of cheddar cheese!"

Amelia giggled. "You could have a gold sandwich!"

"And break your teeth, silly Millie."

"Jane Pain." Amelia shot back. "Georgie Porgie …"

George ignored her. "Can you imagine? What an adventure! I wish I were old enough to go."

"Me, too!" squealed Amelia.

"We *all* wish you could go," said Jane.

At that moment, Mrs. Murdoch came out of the druggist's. "At last I'm done!" She exchanged a few words with George and ushered the girls off to their streetcar stop.

On the way, Emily saw Tom and his father standing with a group of men outside the tobacconist's. She cringed, expecting Tom to give her a nasty look as she walked by, or to mutter something. But he was listening so intently to one of the men that he didn't even notice her.

"Soon as I'm packed, I'm off to the Klondike," Emily overhead the man say. "But listen, fellas, you've got to act fast if you want some of that gold …" The rest of his words were lost in the hubbub of the street.

Gold, gold, and more gold. Emily couldn't believe it. Was she living in the same Victoria? You'd think the gold had been found in Beacon Hill Park, not in some faraway place called the Klondike.

Where exactly was the Klondike? Was it true what she'd overheard, that the sun shone at midnight in the summer, but in winter there was no sunlight at all?

When they reached the car stop, Emily asked her mother if she'd heard anything new in the druggist's.

"Well, yes," Mother said. "Mr. Sinclair wants to sell his store so that he can go to the Klondike. So far, it's only a rumour."

By now, more people were gathering at the stop. Emily listened in on their conversations and tried to sort out the facts from the growing number of rumours.

"… going up north on a bicycle!"

"Mr. Shotbolt, the druggist? He put up a sign saying that Vaseline's a cure for frostbite, and he sold every last jar in minutes."

"Gold fever? It's an epidemic! You bet there's a cure, but it can only be found in the Yukon ..."

By the time they got home, Emily was so muddled with the news that she no longer knew what to think.

"Is the gold rush a true story?" Amelia wondered. "Or is it a fairy tale?"

Jane rolled her eyes. "Of course it's true. People read it in the newspaper and newspapers don't lie."

"Father always brings home a newspaper," Emily reminded them. "When he gets home, we can read about it for ourselves."

Surprisingly, Father did not come home with a newspaper that evening, and at dinner he was unusually quiet. Not quiet, worried, but quiet, excited. As if he were holding a secret he couldn't wait to tell.

While everyone else was talking about the news they'd heard in town or listening to Amelia's story about dressing a friend's cat in doll clothes—since "bossy Emily" wouldn't let her play dress-up with Sam—Emily observed her father. His eyes twinkled. His face glowed. He gazed at Mother with a curious half-smile on his face. And when he caught Emily's eye, he actually winked.

Emily was so taken aback by this uncharacteristic gesture she almost choked on her pudding. Whatever the secret was, it must be something wonderful.

Suddenly, her heart dropped into her stomach. What if Father was thinking of going to the Klondike?

No! She almost laughed out loud. He was a banker, not someone who went off on adventures.

Still, his behaviour was odd. He kept glancing at his watch. Was he expecting someone?

Was a special parcel about to be delivered? Not this late in the day. And there was nothing the girls had to be on time for, except bed, and that was hardly—oh! Perhaps he was waiting to tell Mother something in private. Maybe he was planning to give her a special gift. That had to be it.

The next time he looked at Emily, she gave him a knowing smile and winked—and winked again, to be sure he understood.

She was enjoying the novelty of sharing a secret with her father until Amelia said, "Emily's got something in her eye. She keeps making faces and blinking funny."

"I do not!" Emily glared. Trust Amelia to spoil things.

That night, as soon as she knew that Amelia was asleep, Emily nudged Jane and whispered, "Do you want to hear a secret?"

"Yes!" Jane was instantly awake.

Emily cautioned her to be quiet and told her what she'd observed during dinner. "So now I'm going to sneak downstairs and listen."

"It's not polite to eavesdrop," said Jane. "So if we get caught it was your idea."

Emily agreed. They got out of bed and tiptoed downstairs to the parlour door.

"Eldorado at last!" Father was saying. "Fortune's smiling on us, my dear. A once-in-a-lifetime opportunity."

"You can't be serious!" said Mother.

"Think of it. Here we are, in the right place at the right time, and with a fair bit of grit and perseverance, we'll have a comfortable income. Walsh feels the same way."

"Oh, John! Please ..."

"Let me tell you all about it."

Emily looked at Jane, her heart pounding with

apprehension and dread. If what she was thinking were true, no wonder Father wanted Mother to be the first to know.

They crept upstairs and slipped into bed. "Eldorado has to do with gold, doesn't it?" Jane said quietly. "But what's grit? What did Father mean?"

"Grit means determination. You know what I think?" Emily whispered in Jane's ear.

"But it's so far!" Jane started to cry.

"Be quiet!" Amelia raised her head, took one look at her sister, and said, "Jane, what's wrong?"

"Father's got gold fever!" she sobbed.

Amelia frowned. "He didn't look sick," she said sleepily.

"Not that kind of fever." Emily struggled to hold back her tears. "He's planning to go to the Klondike!"

CHAPTER N.º 5

Emily braced herself. She had joined her parents for breakfast and now looked from one to the other, knowing that the moment had come.

She'd spent half the night fretting about her father, but then another thought had loomed in her mind. What if he were planning to take the whole family to the Klondike? She didn't mind a bit of snow in the winter, but no sunlight? No beaches, no Beacon Hill, no art classes with Miss Carr? She'd hate it! How could she leave Mei Yuk? And what about Alice? They could never be friends if Emily were a million miles away.

After worrying herself into a restless sleep, she'd woken up early and gone downstairs, determined to find out what her father meant to do.

She forced down a mouthful of porridge, swallowed some milk, and boldly said, "I was eavesdropping last night. I'm sorry. I know it was wrong, but ... oh, Father! Please don't go to the Klondike. I'm sure it's a good opportunity and you have lots of grit, but it's too far! And please don't make us go! Who would take care of the garden or do your work at the bank? If you don't want to go alone ..." Her breath caught in a sob. "I'll let you take Sam. But you mustn't stay away too long because he'll forget his training and I'll miss him so terribly ..."

Her voice trailed off as she noticed the amused expressions on her parents' faces. "It's not funny," she said, hurt that they hadn't taken her seriously.

Father leaned over and kissed her cheek. "Dear Emily. Of course it isn't funny. And thank you for offering Sam. It was a kind and thoughtful gesture. But you ought not to eavesdrop, and this is a case in point. You misunderstood what you heard. I'm not going anywhere, certainly not to the Klondike."

Surprised, Emily turned to her mother. "But you sounded so upset."

"I was cautious, dear, and only at first. Once I heard your father's plan, I became rather excited."

"And here's the plan." Father smiled. "Mr. Walsh and I are going to buy Mr. Sinclair's store."

"What?" Emily gaped. "It's true? Mr. Sinclair is selling his store? But he sells hats and clothes, not money. You and Mr. Walsh are bankers."

"Not any more. We're leaving the bank and running our own business. Because even though we're not going north, there are thousands who are, and come next spring there'll be thousands more. And what will they need? Not just hats and clothing, but all sorts of tools and supplies. Everything from candles to gold pans. And where do you think they'll buy them?" He winked.

"From your store?"

"That's right! From Murdoch and Walsh—Outfitters for the Klondike."

The new outfitters had to act quickly, for competition was fierce. Gold-seekers were arriving in droves, from all over the continent, and stores that sold *anything* related to a Klondike expedition were doing a booming business. In a short time, Murdoch and Walsh had increased Mr. Sinclair's stock, bought all manner of food and supplies from the Victoria warehouses, and erected a new sign. Then they placed an announcement in the newspaper saying that they were ready to open.

On the day of the grand opening, Emily accompanied her father to the store. They walked through town, marvelling at how Victoria had transformed since the news of the gold rush. Men dressed in the typical Klondike clothing of canvas coats, knee-high boots, and wide-brimmed hats were now a familiar sight, and the festive atmosphere showed no signs of fading.

Emily had never known her father to be so excited. He had indeed caught gold fever—the stay-at-home kind, thank goodness—and she couldn't help but catch it as well. Especially since she'd been given a special job at the opening.

Murdoch and Walsh—Klondike Outfitters! The store looked very grand with its eye-catching sign stretched across the front. The display windows were filled with items a gold miner would need, from arctic socks, moosehide parkas, and heavy woollen underwear to prospectors' picks and shovels. "Klondike sleighs" hung in rows against the outside wall, and portable "Yukon stoves," especially designed in Victoria, had been placed on the boardwalk.

Emily had been astounded the first time she'd seen a similar display. Sleighs, in Victoria, in summer? Now, such displays were commonplace.

It wasn't long before the first customers began to arrive. Emily's job—better than any chore she could imagine—was to stand at the doorway and offer everyone a candy. George stood beside her. When he wasn't trying to pinch a sweet, he was handing out complete lists of what a Klondike traveller would need.

By mid-morning, Emily was almost out of candy. A steady stream of customers had been entering the store. Many were from the United States. They were buying their outfits in Canada so they wouldn't have to pay duty taxes when they entered the Canadian Yukon. Other customers had purchased their outfits elsewhere but had forgotten a few essential items.

One fellow came out of the store in such high spirits that he gave Emily a handful of his candies instead of taking one of hers. "I can't believe my luck!" he said. Beaming, he held up a copy of *The Complete Works of William Shakespeare.* "A book is hard to come by in the north, and without one to keep me company over the winter, I'd go stark-raving mad."

Another fellow came out with a sleigh

strapped to his back and a hefty bundle of goods. "They've got everything I need in there except for a dog," he said. "Either of you kids know where I can get a good one? One that could pull a sled? I'll pay up to four hundred dollars."

"Emily's got a dandy," George said. "But he's not for sale."

"Then you better keep an eye on him, Miss. There are a lot of desperate men about." So saying, he shifted his load and ambled off.

Emily gave George a worried look. "Nobody would steal Sam ... would they?"

"They might try."

His words were not encouraging. Emily had left Sam at home and wouldn't be back before noon. What if Jane or Amelia took him for a walk and the leash came off, like before? What if someone else tempted him with sausages and tried to lure him away? As soon as the bonbons were gone, she'd go home to make sure everything was all right. And she'd have to train Sam to resist temptation.

"Good morning, Em-ry!"

It was Mei Yuk and Hing. "Welcome to Murdoch and Walsh," Emily said proudly. "Here, have a bonbon."

"Thank you," said Mei Yuk. "Like Chinese New Year, when merchant give special food."

"And read this." George handed Hing a list of supplies. "Everything you need to make the journey in comfort."

"Hing's not going—" Emily's smile vanished when she saw how closely Hing was studying the list. "You're not going to the Klondike, are you?"

"No, I am too old and too smart for new Gold Mountain. But list is good, for practise English."

"Ha! Good luck."

Emily recognized the voice and its snarky tone, and knew right away it was Tom. She moved protectively towards Mei Yuk as Tom approached, his father close behind.

"Come," Hing said to Mei Yuk. "We look in store."

"So *rong*," Tom said with a smirk. Then, to Emily, "Got a candy for me? One without any germs?"

313

Before she could answer, he'd scooped up a handful of bonbons and stuffed them into his pocket.

"Tom!" Mr. Kerr gestured from the doorway. "You coming or not?"

"Yes, sir," Tom said and followed his father into the store.

Emily looked around for Alice, hoping she might have come along, but there was no sign of her or her mother.

Customers continued to arrive throughout the morning, and no one left the store empty-handed. Even friends and neighbours who had dropped by to encourage the new owners found something to buy.

Emily couldn't hide her astonishment when Mr. Sinclair, the former owner, entered the store. A short time later, he came out brandishing a receipt. "Murdoch and Walsh have thought of everything," he announced to a group of men examining the Yukon stoves. "Order an outfit and they'll deliver it straight to the wharf, sealed up and labelled to a T."

"Mr. Sinclair!" Emily burst out. "Are *you* going to the Klondike?"

"Don't sound so alarmed!" he chuckled. "I'm not all that long in the tooth."

Emily blushed. "I'm sorry, I didn't mean it like that. It's just that you're the only person I *know* who's going. When do you leave? Is Mrs. Sinclair going, too?"

"Nope, the missus is staying behind. And I'm off on the *Bristol* in four weeks' time. So if you want to sell Sam, let me know."

"I'd never sell Sam!"

"I know, lass. I'm only teasing."

His comment prompted an even greater urgency to make sure that Sam was safe. Since it was now close to noon and Emily's basket of bonbons was almost empty, she said goodbye to George and her father and hurried home.

She needn't have worried. The moment she turned down her street she saw Sam. He was lying beneath the maple tree, right where she'd told him to stay. "Here, Sam!" she called.

His ears pricked up. With a hearty woof, he bounded over to greet her with such exuberance, you'd think she'd been gone for months.

"I missed you, too!" She hugged him as he slapped wet kisses all over her face, his tail wagging so vigorously it almost knocked her over.

Jane and Amelia were watching from the front verandah. "He wouldn't even come for a walk," Jane said. "Just lay there whining, *Emily, Emily,* all morning long."

"Not *all* morning," Amelia corrected. "We put on his leash and *tried* to take him for a walk, but he wouldn't budge."

"He was as stubborn as a mule," Jane added. "He dug in his feet so hard it was worse than pulling up carrots in the garden."

"I'm glad," said Emily. She told her sisters how worried she'd been and why. "So we have to watch him all the time and not let anyone pet him or give him treats. Except for us."

CHAPTER No. 6

"What now?" Emily muttered crossly. She was hot, sticky, and up to her elbows in raspberries, and Sam was barking down the house. One interruption after another! First the milkman had come. Then Mrs. Sinclair, with a basket of plums. Then the vegetable peddler. Now someone else was knocking on the back door.

"Hush, Sam! I'm coming!"

She'd been pleased at first. To be left on her own with the important task of making jam had made her feel grown-up and responsible. But now she was tired of cooking and stirring and straining, and she wished her mother would hurry up and get home.

She rinsed her hands, shook them dry, and wiped her hair from her sweaty forehead. "I'm coming, Sam! Be quiet!"

The last person she expected to see on opening the door was Alice.

They hadn't seen each other for weeks, and for a moment they just stood there, feeling somewhat shy. Then both started talking at once.

"I would've come—"

"It's been so long—"

They started to laugh. "You first," Emily said.

"I would've come sooner," said Alice, "but I wanted to clean it up first." She turned and looked over the railing.

Emily followed her gaze and gasped. Leaning against the verandah was her bicycle, as shiny as a new coin. The brass bell gleamed, and bright red and blue ribbons had replaced the tattered ones.

"Alice!" she cried. "I can't believe you found it. You, of all people!" She skipped down the stairs and hopped on for a ride around the yard. Sam ran at her side, yapping excitedly.

At the end of the ride, she rang the bell and gave the bicycle a fond pat. "When did you find it?" she asked, joining Alice on the steps. "And where? On the beach? In the park?"

Alice flushed with embarrassment. "I'm sorry to tell you this, but I found it the night before last … in our woodshed. Tom had hidden it in a corner. He said he took it for a joke. He was going to give it right back."

"He should've!" Emily fumed. "And he should've had the courage to bring it back himself. He ought to be punished. When Father tells the police—"

"I told Pa," Alice broke in quietly. "He nearly killed Tom." She looked as if she were about to say more, but she leaned forward instead and scratched Sam behind his ear. "Mei Yuk told me you had a dog."

Emily's mouth fell open. "You were talking to Mei Yuk?"

Alice nodded. "I saw her and Hing at your father's grand opening."

"When were you there? I looked for you after I saw Tom but didn't see you."

"You'd already gone home. Ma had to stop at the druggist's, so I waited for her while Tom and Pa went on ahead."

"And you talked to Mei Yuk?" Emily was astonished. "With your parents right there? And they didn't get after you?"

"They've had a lot of things on their mind lately," Alice said. "I doubt if they even noticed ..." Her voice trailed off and she peered at Emily closely. "Have you cut your head? Your hair's covered with red streaks. And your face—"

"Oh, no! The jam!" Emily bolted inside and snatched the pot off the stove. The mixture had already begun to boil over. "Look at this mess!" she wailed. "Berry stains everywhere, the floor sticks like molasses—I'm doomed! When Mother comes home—"

"Fetch the mop and a bucket," Alice said

calmly. "I've been helping Ma with jams and jellies all week and believe me, I've had lots of practice cleaning up."

Together they set to work. By the time Emily's mother came home, the floor was mopped, the counter tops scrubbed, and the pot scoured, and six jars of raspberry jam were cooling on the counter. The only thing that wasn't gleaming was Emily.

"You've got measles!" Amelia shrieked when she saw her sister's face.

"I know," Emily said happily. "My pinafore's ruined and my hair's too sticky to brush and I don't give a hoot." In one afternoon, she'd regained her bicycle and seen Alice. It was one of the best days of her life.

CHAPTER N.º 7

"Stop whining, Amelia!" Emily *was* rapidly losing her temper. That very morning in Sunday school she'd vowed to be more patient, but she hadn't counted on Amelia.

Why is it always Jane's turn? Stop being so bossy! Why can't we do what I want to do?

It didn't help when Jane kept reminding Amelia that since she was starting school in September, she'd better learn to behave.

The afternoon had started well. The Murdochs had taken the streetcar to the newly built Point Ellice Bridge, then walked along the Gorge

waterway to the Walsh's house. While the grown-
ups were inside celebrating the success of the
new store, George had been entertaining the girls
in the garden.

They'd spent the first hour playing croquet.
Now George was letting them try out his bow
and arrow.

"The target's too far away!" Amelia complained.

"We've already moved it once," said Jane.

"Well it's *still* too far!" She threw down the
arrow and scowled.

"Then don't play!" The others carried on with
their target shooting, determined to ignore her
outbursts.

Finally, George, who'd been a model of
patience, had had enough. "Look, Amelia," he
said. "If you promise to stop whining, we'll do
whatever you want to do."

She stuck out her lower lip. "But you don't
have any dolls to play with. And no cats or dogs
to dress up."

"So think of something else!" Jane said irritably. "Don't be such a baby."

"I'm not!" She furrowed her brow, trying to think of a grown-up game that didn't involve croquet mallets or arrows. "Can it be a 'let's pretend' game, like charades?"

"Yes!" Emily said. "I love charades!"

Amelia was quick to squash that idea. "I said a game *like* charades, and George said I could pick. So let's play ..." She scrunched up her face and thought for a moment. "Let's play gold rush!"

George raised his eyebrows in a question. "All right, but you'll have to tell us how to play."

"Well ... we pretend we're miners. We carry all the pretend supplies we bought from Murdoch and Walsh, and we take George's rowboat to the pretend Klondike."

"We could say it's on Deadman's Island," Emily suggested.

"And we pan for pretend gold!" added Jane.

They all warmed to the idea. Before long, they'd loaded the boat with a shovel and pick for digging, a skillet to use as a gold pan, and two travelling bags stuffed with rocks to serve as their supplies.

George was an enthusiastic rower, and since the island was only a half a mile down the Gorge, they were soon scrambling out of the boat and onto the shore.

Amelia waited until their gear was unloaded and the boat securely fastened, then gave further instructions. "We have to hike along the pretend trail, and everybody has to carry something. George can lead the way because he's a boy."

"Klondike, ho!" he shouted, and off they went.

Up and over the rocks, through a few dense thickets, in and out of the trees—they crossed the small island several times, grumbling about heavy loads, sore muscles, and aching backs, and moaning, "When are we going to get there?"

After the tenth time around, when their groaning was no longer pretend, Emily made a decision. "At last, we've made it!"

"Three cheers for the Klondike!" Jane said. "Hip, hip, hurray!"

"I say we start panning for gold!" said George.

"Me first! It was my idea." Amelia grabbed the skillet from Jane and began filling it with stones.

"Not like that," said Jane. "You scoop up gravel and water and swish it around."

"How do you know?"

"Because I saw a real miner in town showing everyone."

"I'm a miner—"

"A *whiner.*"

"I am not!"

"Stop it!" Emily snapped. "Let George have a turn. He won't waste time squabbling. I'm going to dig for my gold."

She took the shovel and marched into the woods. *Sisters!* They were driving her to distraction. Amelia was getting impossible, and Jane made matters worse by egging her on. She wished someone would pack the pair of them off to the Klondike.

And that Tom, stealing her bicycle! He could go to the Klondike, too.

"Ooof!" She jabbed the shovel into a likely spot of earth. The ground was harder than it looked, but with a fair bit of muscle, some grit, and determination …

It wasn't long before she was panting with exertion. Her face was beaded with sweat and her dress stuck to her back and under her arms. Still, she had a sizable hole to show for her efforts, and the pile of dirt kept growing.

"Horrid, beastly Tom!" She punched out the words with every stab of the shovel. She was swinging back and forth, both feet on the blade, when she heard a burst of muffled laughter. George!

She whirled around and caught him leaning against a tree, shaking with mirth.

"How long have you been spying on me?" She was mortified that he might have heard her venting her anger.

"The whole time!" he hooted. "Why are you doing this? It's only pretend! You're not going to find any gold."

"I know that! I just felt like it." Better to stab at the ground than at her sisters. And stabbing at a pretend Tom didn't feel half bad.

She was about to carry on when she heard a loud splash followed by a chilling scream. "That sounds like Amelia!" Sick with fear, she threw down the shovel and started to run. "I never should have left them!" she cried as the screaming and splashing continued.

When she reached the shore and saw her sisters standing in the water, happily shrieking and splashing each other, her panic turned to anger. "What are you doing?" she yelled.

"Playing gold rush!" Laughing, the girls waded to shore. "Look inside the bags, Em. We found tons of gold. Fools' gold!"

"Yes," Amelia grinned, "and I fell into the creek and pretended I was drowning. Jane rescued me!"

"And then we got hot so we took a little dip."

"A *little* dip? Mother will be furious! Your hair, your clothes—You're drenched! And drowning isn't a game. How *could* you? Don't you remember—" She stopped abruptly, afraid that her anger would give way to tears.

It hadn't been so long ago that the Gorge waterway had echoed with screams. The old Point Ellice Bridge had collapsed, taking a fully loaded streetcar with it. Emily had been one of the passengers, and her memory of the disaster was still vivid, as was the terrifying sensation of being trapped underwater.

"I'll go back for the shovel," said George. "I think it's time we left."

Emily scowled at her sisters. "Now get in the rowboat and be quiet."

The girls protested but did as they were told. "You don't have be so bossy," Jane said. "You're not our mother."

"She's just pretending," said Amelia. "Aren't you, Em?"

"No! And if you think I'm bossy, wait till Mother and Father see you. And they'll blame me, since I'm the oldest."

There was a glum silence as they pushed off the boat and rowed away from the island. After a while, Jane said, "I'm sorry, Em. About the drowning. I wasn't thinking."

"Me, too," Amelia blubbered.

Emily gave them a stern look. "Well, now that you're both sorry, you'd better think of what you're going to tell Mother and Father."

"I'd better do some thinking myself," said George. "Just look at those travelling bags." Having been filled with rocks and gravel, and dragged around the island, the bags were wet and torn and filthy, both inside and out. "They looked fairly new when I took them out of the closet," he added.

The girls exchanged nervous glances. George's sombre tone and the state of the travelling bags made the whole situation worse.

As soon as the girls got home, they were sent to their room. They looked a disgrace after digging and kneeling in the dirt and tramping through the prickly underbrush. Their dresses and stockings were ripped and stained, Jane and Amelia were soaked, and Amelia could have drowned. Emily should have known better. There was no playing with Sam, no supper, and no sweets for a week. There were extra chores and letters of apology written to both sets of parents. All in all, they'd spoiled a splendid afternoon.

George, too, was being punished. Taking his mother's new travelling bags topped the list of his offences. Next came the skillet, scratched beyond any amount of scouring. And since he and Emily were the oldest, they were required to spend two afternoons a week until school started working in the storeroom of Murdoch and Walsh. Whatever wages they might have earned would be used to replace Mrs. Walsh's bags.

Emily paused from writing her apologies and listened to Sam whimpering at the back door. Poor thing. He was missing his playmates after being left alone, inside the house, for most of the day.

Amelia was whimpering, too. "How can I write a pology? I don't know how!"

"That's why you're going to school," Jane said. "So you'll learn. And it's an a–pology, not a *pology*."

"Stop correcting me! You're not my teacher. And I don't want to go to school!" Her voice rose in a wail.

"Come here, Amelia." Emily reached out a hand. "Tell me what you want to say and I'll write it for you. Then you can print your name at the bottom. You know how to do that."

With a loud sniff, Amelia went to Emily and wrapped her chubby arms around her neck. "I'm sorry, Em. It was all my fault. It was a stupid game."

"No, it wasn't," Emily said. "We just got carried away." She smiled. "I actually thought it was fun." And the very sort of game Miss Carr might've played when she was a little girl.

The day after the gold rush game, Emily was allowed to call on Mei Yuk as usual. Mei Yuk was delighted to hear that Emily had to work in her father's store, the way she, Mei Yuk, had to work in her father's restaurant.

At the end of their English lesson, Emily coaxed Sam away from his bone and left in good spirits. She loved Mei Yuk's latest drawing of Sam and couldn't wait to show it to Miss Carr. Maybe Miss Carr would invite Sam to her class. He could pose beside her dog, Watch. They'd be difficult to draw, but much more interesting than the stuffed raven that occupied the studio.

Maybe, once Miss Carr saw how talented Mei Yuk was, she'd invite her to join the class. If that were to happen, Emily wouldn't feel so bad about Mei Yuk's determination not to return to school.

But school was still three weeks away. Emily was thinking of all the things she wanted to do before the end of the holidays, when she saw Tom striding her way.

Her stomach twisted into a knot. She was halfway across the James Bay Bridge, so there were no shops to duck into, and it was too late to turn and gaze at the water, pretending she hadn't seen him. He'd already caught her eye. If he saw that she was avoiding him on purpose, he was sure to say something mean.

Sticks and stones may break my bones but names will never hurt me … She repeated the phrase for courage, but she knew it wasn't true. Words *could* hurt.

When they were face to face, Tom stopped and said, "Hello, Emily. I'm sorry about your bicycle."

Emily was speechless. An apology was the last thing she'd expected from Tom, especially one that sounded sincere. *Suspiciously* sincere.

"I only rode it the once," he said, "and I meant to give it back. But there've been a lot of things happening at home …" He shrugged and smiled sheepishly. "Honest. I'm really sorry. But why aren't you riding it? There's nothing broken, is there?"

"No … it's fine." She spoke cautiously, wondering if he were up to something. "I don't ride it to town because of Sam. He needs a leash with so many people around."

Tom crouched down and ruffled Sam's fur. "Hello, fella!"

Emily winced as Sam wagged his tail and licked Tom's hand, making happy nice-to-meet-you sounds. The traitor!

"Sure is a nice dog. Where did you get him?"

"I found him on the beach. The day you stole my bicycle."

"Borrowed." His eyes narrowed.

The knot in Emily's stomach grew tighter. *Stole* had been the wrong thing to say. If Tom were being sincere, she'd given him the perfect opening to change his tune. "I've got to get home," she said. "Come on, Sam."

"Wait a minute." Tom blocked her way. "You wouldn't want to sell Sam, would you? I need a dog."

"He's not for sale. And why do you need a dog?"

"You ought to know," he taunted. "Little Miss Murdoch, outfitter for the Klondike."

"You're going to the Klondike?" Emily felt such a surge of relief she wanted to whoop with joy. "When?"

"A week from Saturday. Pa and me, we're off on the *Bristol*. So do you see why I need the dog?"

"I suppose so, but you can't have mine." She elbowed her way past Tom and quickened her pace.

"Hey!" Tom caught up and grabbed her arm. "I really am sorry about your bicycle." His tone turned nasty. "Sorry I didn't take it apart and sell it piece by piece. If it hadn't been for Alice snooping around—"

"Let go!" Emily yanked her arm, but the harder she tried to pull away, the tighter he squeezed. "You're hurting me!"

With a fierce growl, Sam lunged at Tom, forcing him to let go.

"Now leave me alone, you thief!" Emily hurled the words in Tom's face and stormed away.

"Call me a thief?" Tom yelled at her back. "What about you? I know who owns that dog! And he's going to want him back!"

For the rest of that day and into the night, Emily worried about Tom's parting words. He'd meant to upset her and he'd succeeded. But it couldn't be true. As Dr. Murphy had suggested, Sam's previous owner had probably thrown the dog overboard on purpose. He wouldn't want him back.

On the other hand, Tom may well have been speaking the truth.

"Oh, Sam," she whispered. He was the best dog in the world. She couldn't imagine losing him.

It was the last thought Emily had before falling asleep.

"*... six bottles of steak sauce, forty boxes* of candles, and eleven bars of soap. There, George. That's another one done." Emily added the items to a gold-seeker's outfit, checked them off a list, and moved on to the next outfit, leaving George to add the flour, salt, sugar, and lard. Other employees handled tools, equipment, clothing, and cases of canned food. Once the outfits were packed, they were set out on the street, ready to be picked up and hauled down to the docks. Then they were loaded onto a ship.

Emily was amazed at the number of boxes, kegs, and crates that made up one outfit. No wonder the ships rode low in the water, looking as though they might sink at any moment.

Her first afternoon at the store was going well. She and George worked side by side, bantering good-naturedly. Both agreed it was the most enjoyable punishment they'd ever had. But they wouldn't dare let on to their fathers.

At the end of their shift, Emily biked home. She had the rest of the afternoon planned. First, a ride around the neighbourhood with Sam. He loved to heel when she rode her bike, and he gave a little woof whenever she rang the bell. After that, she'd go to the park to feed the ducks and maybe call on Alice.

She turned the corner of her street, ringing the bicycle bell to let Sam know she was on her way. She began to feel uneasy when there was no response. And when she saw Amelia trudging across the lawn, Sam's leash in her hand, she knew that something was wrong.

She got off her bike, her heart in her throat. "Amelia …? What happened?"

Amelia's face was wet with tears. "I—I'm sorry," she stammered. "He looked so sad when you left. We only wanted to cheer him up, and he wasn't stubborn like before. He really *wanted* to go for a walk. So—so—" She started to cry.

By this time, Mother had joined them. She ushered them inside where a downcast Jane was waiting and, little by little, the story came out.

"We took Sam to the park," Amelia sniffed.

"I tried to hold on to the leash, but he was too strong," Jane said miserably. "He was chasing the ducks and he saw a squirrel and … and he ran off into the woods."

"We called and called. But he wouldn't come."

"We couldn't find him, but we found the leash." Jane risked a glance at Emily. "So someone …"

"Someone stole my dog!" Emily exploded. "How *could* you?" Her voice shook with tears and rage.

As her mother reached out to comfort her, Emily pushed her away and ran back outside. She got on her bike and pedalled furiously, calling for Sam, stopping only to ask passersby if they'd seen him.

When she got to the park, she asked everyone she met—children feeding the ducks, couples out for a stroll, a group of gold seekers training their dogs to wear a harness and pull a sled. Did they know anything? Did they look guilty?

Several people remembered seeing Sam chasing the ducks and squirrels, but no one knew where he had gone.

She searched the wild part of the park and the slopes of Beacon Hill, frantically calling his name. But there was no sign of him anywhere.

She left the park and biked along Dallas Road to the outer harbour. A gold seeker was the obvious culprit. He could be at the wharves right now, boarding a ship with Sam in tow.

Or it could have been that horrid Tom. She'd stop by his house, search it from top to bottom if she had to—but what if he'd sold Sam? Or what if he did know Sam's former owner? What if Tom had told him where to find Sam, and the brute had lurked around the Murdochs' house and followed Jane and Amelia to the park?

She took a deep breath and told herself to calm down. The hows and whys and what ifs didn't matter. All that mattered was finding her dog.

The last time she'd been at the wharves, she'd felt exhilarated by the highly charged atmosphere. With hundreds of people going off to seek their fortune, the sense of adventure was so strong she'd almost been able to taste it.

Now the scene was a nightmare. Two ships were in the harbour, one taking on cargo, the other taking it off. Throngs of people were milling about—passengers coming and going, getting off one ship or boarding the other, some with dogs, some without; friends and relatives greeting new arrivals or seeing off those who were departing.

She shuddered with despair. How could she hope to find Sam in such a mob?

"SAM!" She strained her voice, praying that it might be heard above the clamour: the hiss of steam winches loading and unloading cargo, the hammering of carpenters, the whinnying, bleating, and barking of horses, sheep, and dogs, the shouts, yells, and cries of people, and—to cap it off—the bawling of a herd of cattle about to be driven onto the northbound ship.

A tap on her shoulder made her jump. She turned, saw Alice, and wailed, "Sam's gone! I think Tom took him!" Between sobs, she told Alice what Tom had said the day before.

"Tom couldn't have taken him," Alice said, shaking her head. "He's been in the house all day, until now. We came to the wharf to meet my Uncle Ted. See that ship?" She pointed to the one that had just finished docking. "Uncle Ted's on it. He's going to the Klondike with Tom and Pa." Without warning, she threw her arms around Emily and burst into tears. "I'm sorry about Sam. But oh, Em! Ma's been in such a state ever since Pa decided he's going to the Klondike. He quit his job and there was a terrible row, and he's taking Tom to keep him out of trouble. I don't know what to do!"

"I'm sure things will be all right." Emily wasn't the least bit sure, but for a moment, she put aside her own worries and tried to reassure her friend. "They'll find some gold and be home in a twinkling. You'll hardly know they've been gone."

"I suppose you're right." Alice blew her nose and wiped her eyes. "You're the best friend I've ever had. You're always right. About Mei Yuk ... and everything."

Emily felt a rush of emotion. With Tom out of the way, there was a good chance that she and Alice could renew their friendship. Mei Yuk might feel brave enough to go back to school. Alice's mother might even soften up a bit, with her husband far away. Life would be perfect. If only Sam were found.

CHAPTER N° 10

Black male dog, white chest and muzzle, tan markings on paws. Well behaved except with ducks and squirrels. Knows how to fetch, say please, *and shake a paw. Loves sausages and bones. Answers to the name of Sam …*

Over the next two weeks, Emily and everyone she knew asked about Sam. Her father placed an ad in the newspaper. Murdoch and Walsh put a large notice in the store window. Nothing helped.

She kept waking up in the night, thinking she'd heard Sam's woof at the back door or the sound of his toenails clicking on the kitchen floor. She got up in the morning hoping to see him lolling on the verandah or snoozing under the breakfast table. Whenever she left the house, she prayed that she'd return to find him dozing under the maple tree, waiting for her.

It didn't help to hear that dogs of all shapes and sizes were selling like hotcakes—or that several neighbours had had a pet stolen from their own backyard. Or that Sam could already be on his way to the Klondike.

She went to the wharves at every opportunity, scanning the crowds, asking questions, calling his name. But time and again, she returned home empty-handed and disheartened.

Then came the day the *Bristol* was due to depart. It was an enormous ship and was said to be carrying the largest assortment of passengers and freight ever to set sail from a Pacific coast port—more than five hundred passengers and dogs, five hundred horses, mules, and oxen, and thousands of tons of cargo.

The wharf hummed with one of the largest crowds Emily had ever seen. Those people who hadn't come by foot had come by carriage, wagon, bicycle—even by canoe or rowboat, like George and Mr. Walsh, who had rowed up from the Gorge. Most had come to see the latest batch of gold seekers on their way, while others had shown up to gawk at the ship. Some, like her parents and sisters, were looking out for a black-and-white dog.

Emily managed to spot a few familiar faces. Mr. Sinclair was leaning over the ship's rail, waving his hat to catch his wife's attention. Alice and her mother were standing at the foot of the gangplank, giving farewell hugs to Tom, Mr. Kerr, and Uncle Ted.

Emily tried to take it all in. How much time was left before the ship set sail? The remaining outfits were being piled into nets, hoisted up from the wharf, and dropped into the ship's hold. The animals had already been herded aboard. But a seemingly endless line of passengers was still waiting on the dock and inching its way up the gangplank.

From her vantage point, she had a good view of the gangplank and paid close attention to the dogs that were accompanying the passengers. Many yapped excitedly, as high-spirited as their owners. Some looked cowed or confused. A few, dragged by ropes, were desperately trying to break free.

Suddenly, Emily's heartbeat quickened. A black dog, halfway up the gangplank, white muzzle, white chest—"Sam!" she bellowed.

Somehow, he heard her above the din. Ears cocked, he looked in her direction, straining against the rope that held him.

Emily burst through the crowd, desperate to save Sam before it was too late. The cargo would soon be loaded and the last passenger would be on board. The crew would haul up the gangplank and untie the moorings. The ship would leave the harbour and Sam would be gone forever.

"Hey! Stop, Miss!" At the foot of the gang-plank, the man taking tickets tried to stop her. "You can't go up there!"

"I'm getting my dog!" Without stopping to argue, she darted away from his outstretched arm and flew onto the gangplank.

The passengers were too busy waving goodbye to the crowd to notice. Ducking under their arms or skirting behind their backs, Emily reached the top of the gangplank and stepped onto the deck.

The crush of people, dogs, and cargo took her breath away. Passengers were standing ten deep at the railing, straining for a last sight of home or loved ones. Those who weren't at the railing swarmed about the deck or the stairways, anxious for the journey to begin.

"Sam!" She meant it as a shout. It came out a croak. He could be anywhere. In the hold, on one of the lower decks, in any number of cabins. It was hopeless.

She pushed through one group after another. Mostly men, a few ladies, even a couple of families with young children. She tugged on coats, interrupted conversations, and pleaded for help. "Have you seen a black dog …"

They'd seen dozens of dogs! But one matching Sam's description? No.

As she was questioning the passengers, a ruckus broke out on the far side of the deck. Loud, angry voices were competing with the snaps and growls of unruly dogs.

One voice rose above the rest. "You can say what you like, but that's not your dog!"

Mr. Sinclair! Emily would have known his Scottish brogue anywhere.

"Well, I'm telling you it is!" another man was shouting. "I bought him fair and square."

"You never did!"

As other voices joined in, Emily struggled to get closer. "Sam!" she cried. "Here, Sam!"

The crowd stepped aside as she ran across the deck.

Hearing her voice, Sam gave a ferocious yank and broke free of the rope. He shot forward and

bounded into her arms, a squirming bundle of lapping tongue and walloping tail.

"There you go, Mister," someone said. "No better proof than that."

When Emily finally looked up, the man who'd either taken Sam or bought him from someone else had disappeared in the crowd. She didn't care. All that mattered—

At that moment, the steam whistle shrieked. The sound set the dogs howling. Any passenger who wasn't already at the rail stampeded over to get as close as they could.

The whistle shrieked again. Then a tremendous cheer erupted, echoed by all those on shore, "KLONDIKE, HO!"

Emily felt a rolling motion and sprang to her feet in alarm.

As she had feared, the gangplank had been raised. The lines had been cast, and the ship was leaving the dock.

CHAPTER N⁰ 11

"It won't be long now," Mr. Sinclair said. He'd alerted the captain to Emily's predicament, the ship had slowed down, and the crew had rigged a cargo net to the winch. Emily and Sam had been lifted inside.

A crewman was going with them, lifebuoy in hand. He gave Emily an encouraging smile. "When we swing the net out over the water, try not to look down."

"You'll be fine, lass," said Mr. Sinclair. "Don't be afraid."

Afraid? Emily was terrified. A few moments

earlier, she'd been gaping at the widening space between the ship and the shore. Now she was inside a cargo net, huddling on a wooden pallet with one arm around Sam and the other holding onto the crewman.

"All set!" he cried.

Mr. Sinclair tipped his hat and grinned. "You're a Murdoch and Walsh special!"

Emily tried her best to return his smile.

"Don't worry," the crewman said kindly. "This net can carry two tons at a time."

Emily gritted her teeth. She felt the net sway as it was hoisted up and over the railing and then— oh! The windblown, heart-stopping swing as it was slowly lowered down to the sea.

In spite of the crewman's warning, Emily looked down. She was amazed to see George and Mr. Walsh rowing towards the ship. As the net came down, Mr. Walsh reached up and grabbed hold. He guided the net into the rowboat and loosened the top. Then he helped Emily and Sam out while George kept the rowboat steady.

Anxious to be on their way, the crew of the *Bristol* was already winching up the crewman. He waved at Emily and said, "That wasn't so bad, was it?"

Emily shook her head and smiled. Then she buried her face in Sam's fur, too overcome to speak.

CHAPTER N° 12

On the Sunday before school started, Murdoch and Walsh organized an outing to Cadboro Bay, a popular spot on the east side of Victoria. Three horse-drawn hay wagons were hired for the occasion, with enough room for employees, families, and friends, as well as several bulging picnic hampers.

Mei Yuk and her brothers were given permission to attend the party and so was Alice. Emily didn't know if this marked a permanent change in Mrs. Kerr's attitude towards the Chinese, but it was a hopeful sign—especially since Mrs. Kerr hadn't made a fuss when Alice announced that Mei Yuk would be returning to school.

The hayride took them through acres of rolling fields and farmlands. Songs were sung in exuberant voices, with each wagonload of singers trying to outdo the others. Sam added to the merriment by barking greetings to every cow, horse, and dog they passed.

When they arrived at the bay, they spread rugs and tablecloths on the sandy beach and set out the picnic. Fried chicken, sausages, roast beef, ham, salad, tomatoes, pickles, preserves, bread rolls, biscuits, lemonade, raspberry cordial—there was enough to feed the navy.

After eating and drinking their fill—at least until tea time—the girls helped Mei Yuk build her first sandcastle. Later, they played hopscotch in the sand, hunted for beach treasures, and splashed in the sea. Later still, the whole party got together for an improvised game of baseball.

As the sun was setting, everyone helped gather wood for a fire. More food and drink came out of the hampers. Lemon tarts, plum cake, almond cake, apple crisp—and leftovers from the earlier meal if anyone was still hungry.

The sky grew dark. A hint of autumn chilled the air. After everyone had wrapped themselves up and found a place near the bonfire, Emily's father stood up, raised his glass of raspberry cordial, and said, "I propose a toast."

Emily groaned inwardly. *Toasts?* They were for Christmas and New Year's, not summer. Stand up, sit down, on and on …

Father seemed to know what she was thinking, for he winked at her and said, "Two toasts only. And no need to raise yourselves, only your glasses." He looked over at George's father. "Walsh, why don't you start?"

"Right!" he said, raising his glass. "To the success of Murdoch and Walsh! May the Klondike be worth its weight in gold."

"To Murdoch and Walsh!" the party chorused.

"And a toast to all of us," Father said. "Thank you for sharing this day."

"To all of us!" the chorus went, with applause and hearty good wishes.

"And that's another summer gone," said Father.

Emily threw her arms around Sam and hugged him. "We'll never have another summer like this one," she said. "Will we, Sam?"

"Woof!"

Everyone laughed.

"I've got a game," Amelia piped up. "You tell everybody your favourite thing that happened this summer. Then you say what you wish for *next* summer. George, you start."

Emily listened as the game passed from one person to another. Surrounded by family and friends, and with Sam at her side, she didn't care what might happen in the future. She couldn't wish for a better time than the present.

1608
Samuel de Champlain establishes the first fortified trading post at Quebec.

1759
The British defeat the French in the Battle of the Plains of Abraham.

1812
The United States declares war against Canada.

1845
The expedition of Sir John Franklin to the Arctic ends when the ship is frozen in the pack ice; the fate of its crew remains a mystery.

1869
Louis Riel leads his Métis followers in the Red River Rebellion.

1871
British Columbia joins Canada.

1755
The British expel the entire French population of Acadia (today's Maritime provinces), sending them into exile.

1776
The 13 Colonies revolt against Britain, and the Loyalists flee to Canada.

1837
Calling for responsible government, the Patriotes, following Louis-Joseph Papineau, rebel in Lower Canada; William Lyon Mackenzie leads the uprising in Upper Canada.

1867
New Brunswick, Nova Scotia and the United Province of Canada come together in Confederation to form the Dominion of Canada.

1870
Manitoba joins Canada. The Northwest Territories become an official territory of Canada.

1783
Rachel

Timeline

1885
At Craigellachie, British Columbia, the last spike is driven to complete the building of the Canadian Pacific Railway.

1898
The Yukon Territory becomes an official territory of Canada.

1914
Britain declares war on Germany, and Canada, because of its ties to Britain, is at war too.

1918
As a result of the Wartime Elections Act, the women of Canada are given the right to vote in federal elections.

1945
World War II ends conclusively with the dropping of atomic bombs on Hiroshima and Nagasaki.

1873
Prince Edward Island joins Canada.

1896
Gold is discovered on Bonanza Creek, a tributary of the Klondike River.

1905
Alberta and Saskatchewan join Canada.

1917
In the Halifax harbour, two ships collide, causing an explosion that leaves more than 1,600 dead and 9,000 injured.

1939
Canada declares war on Germany seven days after war is declared by Britain and France.

1949
Newfoundland, under the leadership of Joey Smallwood, joins Canada.

1896
Emily

1885
Marie-Claire

1917
Penelope

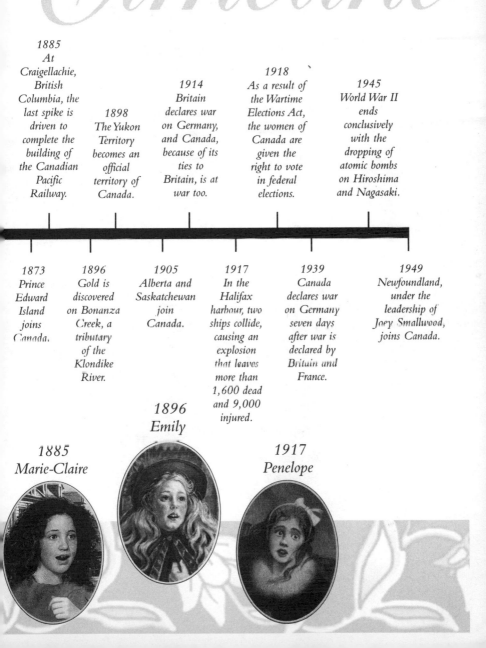